STAR WARS
THE HIGH REPUBLIC

MISSION TO DISASTER

JUSTINA IRELAND

ILLUSTRATIONS BY
PETUR ANTONSSON

DISNEP

LUCASFILM
PRESS

LOS ANGELES·NEW YORK

© & TM 2022 Lucasfilm Ltd.

All rights reserved. Published by Disney • Lucasfilm Press, an imprint of Buena Vista Books, Inc. No part of this book may be reproduced or transmitted in any form or by any means, electronic or mechanical, including photocopying, recording, or by any information storage and retrieval system, without written permission from the publisher. For information address Disney • Lucasfilm Press, 1200 Grand Central Avenue, Glendale, California 91201.

Printed in the United States of America

First Edition, January 2022

10 9 8 7 6 5 4 3 2 1

FAC-034274-21323

ISBN 978-1-368-06800-0

Library of Congress Control Number on file

Reinforced binding

Design by Soyoung Kim and Scott Piehl

Visit the official *Star Wars* website at: www.starwars.com

STAR WARS
THE HIGH REPUBLIC

The tragic events of the Republic Fair have galvanized the galaxy. The Jedi and the Republic have gone on the offensive to stop the marauding NIHIL. With these vicious raiders all but defeated, Jedi Master AVAR KRISS has set her sights on LOURNA DEE, the supposed Eye of the Nihil, and has undertaken a mission to capture her once and for all.

But unbeknownst to the Jedi, the true leader of the Nihil, the insidious MARCHION RO, is about to launch an attack on the Jedi and the Republic on a scale not seen in centuries. If he succeeds, the Nihil will be triumphant and the light of the Jedi will go dark.

Only the brave Jedi Knights of STARLIGHT BEACON stand in his way, but even they may not be enough against Ro and the ancient enemy that's about to be unleashed. . . .

STAR WARS TIMELINE

THE HIGH REPUBLIC

FALL OF THE JEDI

REIGN OF THE EMPIRE

THE
PHANTOM
MENACE

ATTACK OF
THE CLONES

THE
CLONE WARS

REVENGE OF
THE SITH

THE
BAD BATCH

SOLO:
A STAR
WARS STORY

AGE OF
REBELLION

THE NEW
REPUBLIC

RISE OF THE
FIRST ORDER

REBELS

ROGUE ONE:
A STAR WARS
STORY

A NEW HOPE

THE EMPIRE
STRIKES BACK

RETURN OF
THE JEDI

THE
MANDALORIAN

RESISTANCE

THE FORCE
AWAKENS

THE LAST JEDI

THE RISE OF
SKYWALKER

Avon Starros did not bounce. The only daughter of Senator Ghirra Starros and youngest member of the illustrious Starros Clan of Hosnian Prime did not jump for joy or leap in excitement. She was, in a word, a scientist.

But Avon found herself bouncing down the hallway all the same.

"Really? Today? I can finally try synthesizing a Starros crystal today?" Avon said, following her mentor, Professor Glenna Kip, toward the lab in Port Haileap. The outpost wasn't much more than a rest stop for the ships going to and returning from the farthest edges of the galaxy, but it was also home to the research lab of Professor Kip, a well-known scientist.

"Yes, today," Professor Kip said, a smile splitting the silver-lined green of her face. "You can prepare your samples, and we'll get to it after the midday meal."

"Yes! Thank you, Professor Kip. I'm going to go get everything ready now, and I'll see you after lunch."

Avon hustled down the hallway toward the lab. After months spent memorizing the basic structure of kyber crystal molecules, analyzing the atoms, and testing energy refraction and the like, Avon was finally about to do the one thing she had wanted to do from the first moment she had stolen Padawan Imri Cantaros's broken lightsaber: make a reproduction of a kyber crystal.

The construction of the lightsaber seemed relatively straightforward, and Avon couldn't help wondering if it was possible that maybe the kyber crystals could be used for different applications. After all, she had no use for a laser sword—she was a scientist, not a Jedi—but it would be nice if perhaps there was some way to use a kyber's focusing abilities to harness the ambient energy of space.

With so much random radiation and the like just floating around, could they somehow duplicate the kyber's structure to direct that energy to power entire planets?

Avon thought so, even if no one else did.

It had taken months to convince her mentor that a project such as a simulated kyber crystal could be useful and worthwhile, and although Professor Kip had tried over and over again to get Avon to turn her attention to the natural sciences, such as the crop yield project she was currently pursuing, Avon didn't really care about making plants grow faster or making herds produce more offspring. She wanted to understand power, and how things like tibanna could be stretched further and more efficiently, or even replaced altogether. After all, the galaxy was expanding, and fuel would be necessary to keep supplies running to the frontier. Avon knew that because it was something her mother talked about regularly on their weekly calls.

So, after months of diagramming the crystal's structure, making copious notes, and gathering all the relevant research available on kyber—most of it requested from the Jedi Temple on Coruscant with the help of Professor Kip— Avon was finally ready to test out her theory.

Professor Kip would not return for another hour or so, but once Avon got to the lab, she very quickly prepared it for her experiment. The kyber was nestled in its holder, and the Lonnigan duplicating apparatus was all set up. The only thing missing was Professor Kip. So Avon began skipping circles in the lab, waiting for her mentor to return.

Skipping was not bouncing, but it was very close.

Avon checked the time once more. Her stomach grumbled at her, and she was half considering going to grab some lunch from the noodle cart.

That was when the explosions started.

Avon ran to the door of the lab and opened it, peeking out into the rest of the Port Haileap complex. The Jedi and every Republic official lived in the compound, and there were a few rooms for transient guests, as well. But there was no good reason for any of the noise that Avon heard.

The sounds of blaster fire and far-off explosions were growing louder, with shouting and screaming providing a background to the echoes of battle. A young Togruta ran toward Avon, the other girl's striped head tails swinging as she moved.

"Talia! What's going on?" Avon yelled. Talia was another student of Professor Kip's, though her interests tended more toward the plants and natural sciences that Professor Kip preferred.

"It's the Nihil! They're attacking Port Haileap."

"Are you sure?" Avon asked, dread tightening her belly. The Nihil were supposed to be defeated. The Jedi and the Republic had rousted the space pirates from every single hidey-hole in the galaxy. But that seemed to be false, since someone was definitely attacking Haileap.

"I saw the Strike ships fly in," Talia said. "They looked like Nihil."

Avon waved Talia into the lab. "Come on, we can hide in here," she said.

"In here?" Talia asked, sliding to a stop in front of the door to the lab. "They'll find us."

"Nonsense. We can hide in one of the supply cupboards."

The girls entered the lab, locking the door behind them. Along the back wall was a line of cupboards used to store the numerous items needed in a working lab, and Avon pointed to the closet on the far left of the line of doors. "You hide with the lab coats. I'll squeeze into the droid closet. Jay-Six is on loan to Master Boffrey today, so it's totally empty."

Talia nodded and dashed into her spot. Avon was right behind her, but then she realized that she'd forgotten her kyber crystal, still strapped to the analysis plate of the machine.

She couldn't leave that behind, could she?

As Avon ran toward the machine, the sounds of fighting outside of the room grew closer. In the hallway triumphant hooting and hollering echoed, and heavy footsteps approached the lab. She had to hurry.

Avon reached into the machine and grabbed the crystal just as the door exploded inward, forcing her to duck behind the examination table to avoid the debris. Standing in the doorway was a human man, his skin pale under the blue paint smeared haphazardly across his body.

"Well, hello there, little sprout," he said, his voice gravelly and a bit muffled by the mask he wore. Behind him purple smoke billowed, the fog of war as the Nihil called it, a gas that could confuse and was toxic to most organisms in the galaxy. The man's mask had a rebreather attached, so there was no chance that he would inhale any of the poisonous gas, but Avon was not so prepared.

The kyber crystal in her hand, Avon looked around the lab for her options. The man blocked her one chance of escape, but there were lots of things that could be useful in the lab. She just had to come up with a logical plan of attack.

But she didn't have the chance. The Nihil leveled his blaster and fired at Avon, the stun blast hitting her right in the chest, knocking her backward off her feet.

"Nighty night," the Nihil said.

Vernestra Rwoh, Jedi Knight, master to Padawan Imri Cantaros, needed a nap.

"Come on, Vern, one more round! I think I'm finally getting the hang of it!" called Imri from the middle of the canyon, where he hung in midair after missing the jump. Vernestra was holding Imri aloft with the Force, and she very carefully set him down on the ground beside her. That was the thirty-third time she had caught him. She was exhausted.

Since Imri had become Vernestra's Padawan after the *Steady Wing* disaster, they hadn't had a lot of opportunities for controlled practice in the field. Between fighting the Drengir and then the Nihil and going to Coruscant to help Master Stellan, they'd been too busy to just take a day and practice the fundamentals. But now the Nihil leader, the mysterious Eye, was on the run, and the Republic and the Jedi had finally restored safety to the frontier and the hyperspace lanes.

Vernestra had decided it was beyond time that Imri had some more formalized instruction. They'd traveled to Kirima to give Imri a chance to practice a few different techniques, such as jumping longer distances and leaping great heights. Vernestra thought it would be a good place to finally practice the skills they hadn't yet had a chance to explore.

Imri was, as usual, enthusiastic but maybe not the best at using the Force for great feats of strength. He was fantastic at creating bonds and using the Force to soothe emotions, something that Vernestra had worried over initially but now saw as just the way Imri interpreted the will of the Force. Working with the younger boy had been as much a learning experience for Vernestra as it had been for Imri. Vernestra had become a Jedi Knight at the tender age of fifteen, much younger than most, and now at nearly eighteen she realized that she had learned much more from having a Padawan than from any other part of her life as a Jedi. Imri was to be thanked for that.

But she was really, really tired of catching the boy before he plunged to his death.

"I feel like Master Sskeer has a different idea of the best training for a Padawan than I do," Vernestra said, eyeing the canyon before them once more. It had been Master Sskeer who had suggested the training location, and his former Padawan Keeve had laughed when Vernestra had asked her about her experience training with him on Kirima.

"Oh, Imri will find it unforgettable. Trust me," she had said with a grin. Vernestra had gotten the impression that she'd meant that in a bad way, but Imri was having a blast.

"Okay, one more time. And then we need to find some lunch," Vernestra said, her middle achingly empty. "Ready?"

Imri squared his shoulders and sank into a crouch. "Ready."

Vernestra ran toward Imri, using the Force to push off the ground so each step became explosive. She sped past him, toward the looming edge of the cliff and the canyon beyond. At the last possible moment she jumped, using the

Force to carry her up and across, her jump far more powerful than anything an average being could accomplish on their own.

She skidded to a stop on the other side and turned to see Imri grinning after her. "All right, it's your turn!" she yelled back, cupping her hands around her mouth to make sure that her voice could carry across the distance.

Imri began to run toward the edge of the ravine, and Vernestra prepared to catch him if he needed her to. It was more likely than not. They had been on Kirima the whole day, and he had yet to make the jump.

This would be the time when he did. Vernestra could feel it.

Imri reached the edge of the canyon and launched himself across, his arms windmilling as he flew through the air. Vernestra grinned at the trajectory and speed of his jump. He was going to make it.

Kirima faded away, and Vernestra was suddenly watching a man dressed as a Nihil shooting Avon, the girl falling to the ground in a laboratory Vernestra had never before seen. A figure loomed over her, and Vernestra reached out, trying to help her friend.

"Oof!"

Imri slammed into Vernestra, and they both went tumbling backward into the dirt. Vernestra groaned as Imri scrambled to his feet.

"Vern! Are you okay? Did you see that? I made it! I did it!" Imri jumped up and down, punching the air in excitement.

"Ugh, yes, you did. Excellent job," Vernestra climbed to her feet with a frown, dusting herself off as she did.

"Vern? What's wrong? You're troubled." Imri's ability to read the emotions of those around him was stronger than most Jedi's, and he'd become a valuable asset to diplomatic missions because of it. It no longer overwhelmed him since he now had a number of targeted meditations he could use when the emotions of others became too much. Vernestra was proud that Imri had been able to find a way to embrace his abilities instead of resisting them. She had helped, but the accomplishment was still due to his hard work. It was one of her favorite things about her Padawan. He just didn't give up.

She wished she could be as brave as him.

"As you jumped I had a vision," Vernestra said.

Imri's mouth fell open. "Here? But I thought that usually only happened in hyperspace for you."

"Yeah, which is why it was so alarming. I wonder if it's because it was somehow more personal? I saw Avon, and she looked to be in danger."

"Do you think something happened to Port Haileap?" Imri asked. The distant planet Haileap had been their home for a while when Vernestra had been a new Knight and Imri had been Padawan to Jedi Master Douglas Sunvale, who had perished in the devastation of the *Steady Wing* explosion. They both still had a number of friends on Haileap, and the thought that something terrible had happened there was not an easy one. "Do you think it could be the Nihil?"

Vernestra shook her head. "I'm not sure how. The person was dressed like the Nihil, but the efforts of the Jedi and the Republic have all but eliminated them. It might be nothing at all. Maybe I just need some water."

Imri's expression went hard. "We should send a call back to Haileap, just in case."

Vernestra and Imri hiked back to their ship, which was only a couple of kilometers away. As they walked Vernestra tried not to let her thoughts run wild. There was no benefit in that.

When they reached the ship, Imri's expression had gone from worried to positively distraught. "Imri, don't let your worry take hold of you. Accept it and let it wash over you and propel you into action," Vernestra said with a smile that she hoped revealed none of her own concern. Was that sudden connection to Avon a vision of the future or a call for help? In the past couple of months Vernestra had begun having visions in hyperspace once again, a talent she'd thought lost to her days as a Padawan. But her visions had led her and Imri to Mari San Tekka, a hyperspace navigator being monstrously preserved by the Nihil for her ability to calculate seemingly impossible yet perfectly safe hyperspace routes at incredible rates. After the woman had passed on, Vernestra had thought her visions might cease, but she'd found that instead of stopping they'd changed. The flashes she got didn't make much sense, but she'd taken to noting them in a small recording rod she kept in one of her belt pouches. Perhaps one day she would understand them better. For now, she kept them to herself.

But she was left with frustration. Had her visions been pointing her to whatever Avon was now wrapped up in?

She kept seeing fire rain down on a beautiful green-and-blue planet, people calling for help and shouting in despair. She'd tried going through the databanks to see if there had been any reported disasters of the magnitude she had seen on just such a planet, but she had not discovered anything. Which made Vernestra think that perhaps it hadn't happened yet.

But that meant there was even more reason for concern.

Vernestra had thought this excursion to Kirima would help clear their minds, but here they were, heading back with even more worries plaguing their thoughts. Fighting the Nihil had taken its toll, and Vernestra couldn't help thinking that Imri might be right. Haileap could truly be in danger.

They boarded the small ship they'd been allowed to borrow, the *Wishful Thinking*. The Jedi quartermaster on Starlight Beacon, Master Nubarron, still hadn't forgiven Vernestra for crashing not one but two of their prized ships, but they were at least letting her have smaller skiffs once more when she promised Imri would do most of the flying. It was a good compromise. Imri was a capable pilot.

She and Imri entered the shuttle and got a quick drink

of water to wash the dust from their throats, and then Imri powered up the shuttle while Vernestra played the waiting message.

"Jedi Knight Vernestra Rwoh and Padawan Imri Cantaros," the message began. The likeness of Jedi Master Estala Maru, the Jedi who ran the control center on Starlight Beacon and coordinated the activities of all who lived there, flashed before them as the holomessage played. "We've had an alert from Master Jorinda that there was a possible Nihil attack in Port Haileap and there have been a number of casualties. Since you are the closest, Starlight Beacon is asking for you to respond. Please go to the outpost, assess the damage, and report back. Confirm receipt of message."

Vernestra sent back confirmation and nodded to Imri. "Well, that saves us a call to Port Haileap. Let's head straight there. I'll grab a couple of ration packs out of the back and we can eat while we fly."

Imri bit his lip as the shuttle lifted off the ground. "I hope Avon is okay."

"Me too," Vernestra said, but she had a creeping feeling that her vision had been the real thing.

CHAPTER THREE

Avon woke on a ship, the stink of metal and fuel exhaust welcoming her back to reality. She sat up and rubbed her eyes, relieved to find her hands were unbound.

Her head hurt, and she tried to calmly think about the last thing she remembered. The lab. Finally getting permission to simulate a version of Imri's kyber crystal. And then the fog of war, and a Nihil standing in the doorway.

A very promising day flushed right down the vac tube.

Avon patted the side pocket of her trousers and felt the familiar weight of Imri's kyber crystal. She still had it. Not that there was much she could do with it, but at least it was something working in her favor.

Avon took in her surroundings. She was lucky to be alive, and that caused a curious sort of panic to rise in her chest. The Nihil weren't known for taking prisoners, yet there Avon was in a ship's cargo hold, judging from the scent of kava berries coming from a nearby crate.

"Hey, she's awake!"

The voice was young, and Avon turned to find a boy peering at her, an Umbaran judging by his pale bluish skin and sharp features.

"Hello. I'm Avon," she said. She almost said her last name, but then she hesitated. The kid didn't look like a Nihil, but what was he doing on this ship if he wasn't one of them? Also, Starros was a very recognizable last name. Her mother, Ghirra Starros, was the senator from Hosnian Prime, and that afforded her some measure of fame. Avon didn't think anyone knew who she was. The last time she'd been kidnapped, they'd told her to speak into a holo-recorder so they could demand a ransom, but this time she seemed to have been just dumped with some other kids. If the Nihil didn't know Avon was a senator's daughter and weren't keeping her alive to ransom her, which seemed to be the most logical assumption since she wasn't alone in the cargo hold, then why was she there? It was a mystery that required investigation, and Avon was quite okay with that. She'd rather not be kidnapped at all, but her scientific mind put that to the side and tried to focus on the facts.

"I'm Krylind," said a Kage girl with pale green skin, long black hair twisted up in twin braids, and pink eyes with black irises.

"Where are we?" Avon asked. Her body was sore, most likely the aftereffects of the gas. Or maybe the stun blast the Nihil man had hit her with. The gas was the more likely culprit, though. She'd read a number of reports about the Nihil's fog of war, mostly because Avon found it fascinating how science could be used for so many different purposes, and not all of them good.

"We're on a Nihil ship. They brought you on board after they stopped in Port Haileap. I'm Liam from Hetzal, and Petri is from Hynestia," said another boy, a pale human with a shock of auburn hair. The Umbaran, Petri, gave Avon a tiny wave.

"What do they want with us?" Avon asked. She stood

and walked around the small area, inspecting it. Locked crates, a few wrapped packets of food, and a pile of blankets, most likely for them to wrap themselves in when they slept.

It looked like a plan for the worst sleepover ever.

"We don't know. I thought they were going to eat us, but it seems like they have other food," Petri said, hugging his knees.

"Why would they eat us when they have an entire cargo hold full of supplies? It doesn't make any sense," said Krylind, sniffling. "I heard that the Nihil were destroyed by the Jedi, but then they came to my village and burned it to the ground. And there wasn't a single Jedi to save us."

"The Jedi can't be everywhere at once," Avon said. "If you were in trouble and the Jedi knew, they would've helped."

"How do you know?" Liam demanded, his bottom lip trembling. There was a bruise on the boy's cheek, an angry purple thing that looked like it hurt.

"I know Jedi. Two of them. And the Jedi have saved my life lots of times," Avon said matter-of-factly, because it was true. "If we can get a message to Starlight Beacon, I'm sure that they'll send someone to save us."

"Oh yeah, and how are we going to do that?" Krylind asked, sniffling. "You have a comlink in your pocket?"

Avon looked around the cargo hold. "No, I don't. But maybe we can slice into their comm system from here."

The other kids sat up, suddenly interested in Avon, and not just because she was new. She climbed to her feet and started digging through the open crates, the locked ones impossible to open without her usual kit. If J-6 had been there she would've been able to easily slice into any system. Of course, if J-6 were there she would've probably gotten them in bigger trouble. Avon's dialogue upgrade to the droid had the unintended effect of making her a little too honest at times, and Avon had discovered that the last thing most people wanted was a brutally honest droid.

But that was no matter. Avon was in her element. There was a problem with a possible solution, and she just had to figure out how to make it happen.

As she dug through the boxes, pulling forth pieces that could be useful, the other kids relaxed a little, their tears drying and their fearful expressions melting into curiosity. That made Avon relax a little, as well.

It was a far better option than giving in to the terror that threatened to overwhelm her.

"Can we help?" Liam said, and Avon nodded. The rest of the kids huddled close, and as Avon began to ask them questions, real questions about the pirates and their routines, a plan began to blossom in her mind.

They would get a message to Vern and Imri, and once they did they would be saved. Surely it could be that easy?

Avon had to believe it could, and not just for her own sake, but for the sake of everyone else, as well.

FOUR

Imri made record time to Port Haileap from the Mid Rim planet of Kirima. Vernestra didn't even try to fly the shuttle, content to let Imri take the yoke while they ate vac-packed sandwiches. She didn't have any of her funky hyperspace visions during the jump, and that was unfortunate.

It would've been nice to have the Force tell her that Avon was okay.

As soon as they entered the atmosphere above Port Haileap, it was clear that something terrible had happened. The marblewood forest around the docking bays was aflame, aerial firefighting droids skimming above the treetops in an attempt to put out the blaze. A long scar marred the thickest part of the forest, the wreckage of a ship buried in the dirt a few kilometers away.

"Whoa," Imri said, pointing to the crash site. "Does that look like a Nihil ship?"

"It looks like a Vector," Vernestra said, voice low. How had the Nihil taken out a Jedi ship? The Vectors could be flown only by Jedi, and the vessels were better than just about any other ship out there. Jedi rarely crashed, and it had to have been a pretty significant battle for such a sight.

They followed the docking instructions to park the *Wishful Thinking* in a relatively intact part of the yard and quickly disembarked.

"Ahhhh, look at the noodle cart!" Imri said, holding his head when his eyes landed on the smoking ruins of the food stand. His expression immediately shifted into embarrassment. "Sorry, I know there's a lot of other damage. But that was my favorite place to eat."

"Let's hope the vendor made it away safely," Vernestra said, patting her Padawan's arm.

A Jedi Master approached them as they walked off the shuttle.

"Thank the Force you're here. How did you get here so quickly from Starlight Beacon?"

Vernestra shook her head. "We weren't on Starlight. Imri and I had taken a trip to Kirima for a bit of falling practice, but we came here as soon as we got the call."

Jedi Master Jorinda Boffrey, a Delphidian with ridged midnight-black skin, nodded. "Well then, the Force knew we would need you. I'm glad you're here."

"What happened?" Imri asked, his face twisted with horror as he took in the docking yard. Port Haileap—a way station that welcomed travelers before they departed to the edges of navigable space, usually well-appointed and full of visitors—was a smoking ruin filled with people who looked lost as they cleaned up debris and rebuilt damaged storefronts.

"There were about five or six ships that came in all at once. We thought that was unusual, but they didn't look like Nihil vessels, so Kohta and I were not overly alarmed."

"Kohta?" Vernestra asked, not recognizing the name.

"Jedi Knight Kohta Jarik. The Vector you saw in the forest was hers. She fought valiantly," Master Jorinda said, her expression pained. "But there were too many of them, and they were everywhere. Everyone who could fight was engaged with the Nihil, and then just as quickly as they arrived, they were gone. But we were lucky to have only a few casualties. I've called Starlight Beacon for help with the cleanup and to let them know that this was a Nihil attack. I thought the pirates had been dealt with, which was part of our surprise when they struck. That and only a couple of the ships had Path engines, which seemed odd."

"The Nihil are adapting," Vernestra said. The Path drives had once allowed the Nihil to jump into hyperspace in places where there were no beacons or where a planet's mass shadow should've prevented leaping into hyperspace. But without Mari San Tekka, the old woman who was able to calculate jumps and somehow see all the possible Paths through hyperspace, the drives were unreliable. They could either jump safely to hyperspace or explode spectacularly, so some of the Nihil had taken to using regular hyperdrives once more.

But Master Jorinda was right. The Nihil were supposed

to be a non-issue at this point. The Republic and the Jedi were on the trail of their leader, Lourna Dee, and Vernestra couldn't understand why they'd attacked Port Haileap. It seemed like an unnecessary risk when the Nihil were already whittled thin by Republic peacekeeping forces and the Jedi.

"Master Jorinda, have you been able to take a head count?" Vernestra asked. "While Imri and I were training I had a vision. Of a friend of ours, one of Professor Kip's assistants."

"And you're wondering if your friend is hurt? Well, I don't think she's in the infirmary, but feel free to check. Although I would appreciate some help with this cleanup. It would go much faster with extra Jedi."

"Vern, I can stay and help clean up while you go check," Imri said.

"Okay, I'll be right back," Vernestra said, moving off while Master Jorinda instructed Imri in his task. Vernestra knew the way to the infirmary. Port Haileap had been her first assignment as a brand-new Jedi Knight, and even though it had been only a little more than a year since she left, it felt strange to walk through the corridors of the place. She was so different now than she had been when she first arrived on the planet, and she experienced a curious feeling as she walked through familiar buildings that had changed just slightly, like she was two versions of herself at once: the young Knight who had once been eager to report for duty and the battle-savvy Knight who had a Padawan and was regularly called to fight for the light. She wondered what her previous self would say about this version. Was this who she thought she'd turn out to be when she first got to Haileap? Would her past self be disappointed to meet a Vernestra who spent more time fighting than communing with the Force? She didn't know.

"Well, aren't you a sight for sore photoreceptors," said someone with an all-too-familiar voice.

J-6—part childcare droid, part security droid, all attitude—clomped down the hallway toward Vernestra, and Vernestra's immediate response was relief. If anyone knew where Avon was, it would be her minder.

"Jay-Six! I'm looking for Avon. Where is she?"

"Not the infirmary," the droid said, her digitized voice huffy, like she was put out by having to walk all over looking for her charge. Avon had made some updates to the droid's operating system, and she had never been the same since. Her speech patterns were distinct from most other droids, with an edge of sarcasm that any other owner would have seen as a fatal flaw but that Avon somehow found absolutely delightful.

"Have you checked the lab? Where's Professor Kip?" Vernestra asked. Professor Glenna Kip, Avon's mentor, seemed to be the one person who wasn't constantly frustrated by Avon's intellectual pursuits or the chaos they sometimes caused.

"I haven't seen Professor Kip since the fighting. By the way, I finally got to use my blasters just now, and I can honestly say it was one of the best times I have logged in my databank. Those Nihil scum better not return to Haileap, or I am going to enjoy blasting them once more."

Vernestra looked askance at J-6 but said nothing. Was this another part of Avon's tinkering coming to the forefront, or was it just the droid's nature? Vernestra didn't want to know.

They reached the lab, the sight of blaster burns on the wall an ominous sign. The door was destroyed, the metal creating an angry-looking jagged opening, and sounds of movement came from the room beyond. Were there still Nihil in Haileap?

Vernestra drew her lightsaber, the blade glowing purple in the space, and one of the many blasters tucked away within J-6 appeared, held in a mechanical arm that emerged from the droid's chest plate.

Vernestra looked to J-6 and nodded. She thought they were going to sneak in on the count of three or something similar.

But J-6 immediately charged through the blasted door with a battle cry.

"Was that necessary?" Vernestra asked, following along and holstering her lightsaber when it became clear the lab beyond was empty.

"My sensors picked up movement inside, so I thought I might get the chance to use the large blaster. Sadly there's nothing here," J-6 said, the mechanical arm and blaster retreating back into the droid's chest cavity. "But the blaster . . . impressive, isn't it?"

"Quite. Jay-Six, just how many blasters do you have now?"

The droid made a sound that was uncomfortably close to a laugh. "I would rather not say. Avon convinced her mother to give me an upgrade after the disaster at the Republic Fair on Valo some months ago, and let's just say I have quite the arsenal. I'm not picking up any of Avon's life signs in here, but there is someone in that cupboard over there."

Vernestra entered the lab, noting the spent gas canister someone had kicked into a corner. This looked to be the place from her vision, and a creeping unease unfurled in her middle. The Nihil had definitely been there, but whether Avon had been in the lab at the time, that wasn't clear. But someone *was* behind the nearest cupboard door, huddled and afraid, and Vernestra called out to them.

"Hey, you can come out now. It's safe. I'm a Jedi and I'm here to help," she said, standing right in front of the door. "I know you hid because there were some scary things happening, but it's over now. You're safe."

Vernestra waited, and eventually the door slid open a tiny bit. A Togruta girl of nine or ten stuck her head out, her face streaked with tears.

"Are you really a Jedi?" the girl asked. Vernestra answered the question by pulling her lightsaber free from her holster and levitating it above her hand.

"Whoa," the girl said, eyes wide. "Avon said she had Jedi friends, but I thought she was making it up. You must be Vern."

Vernestra opened her mouth to correct the girl's use of the hated nickname, but then she smiled and nodded. "I am Vern. What's your name?"

"I'm Talia. I work with Professor Kip on botany and agricultural sciences. Avon was in here working when the Nihil came, and she thought we should hide in here, in one of the cupboards."

"Where is Avon now?" J-6 asked.

Talia shook her head, her striped head tails shimmying with the movement. "I don't know. After I got into the closet there were voices, and then I heard Avon coughing." Talia's eyes fill with tears once more, and she sniffed.

"I think the Nihil took her."

CHAPTER FIVE

Avon sat on the floor of the cargo hold of the Nihil ship and tried to look sad. Bored. Anything but anxious and clever.

They all sat waiting for the moment when the Nihil would bring them the last meal of the day. Avon had gone over the schedule with the other kids time and time again, until the plan had been airtight. The others, Liam, Krylind, and Petri, kept exchanging looks among one another. Avon could tell they didn't think her idea would work, but that was only because they didn't know her. Avon had an 87.3 percent rate of success when it came to hijinks and varying shenanigans. She could do this, and they would see just how brilliant her plan was.

There was a scraping noise at the door and swearing on the other side. Then the cargo bay door slid open with a shriek, courtesy of the goop Avon had jammed into the mechanism.

"Oy, what's the big idea?" said the Trandoshan who entered, a box of rations in his arms. For a heartbeat Avon thought maybe he was Master Sskeer, but this Trandoshan had a mean, snarly look that was totally different from Master Sskeer's sort of growly look.

Avon gave a quick nod, and her plan snapped into action. Petri and Liam pushed the Nihil to the side while Avon burst through the open door, running full tilt down the hallway, her boots echoing on the metal floor as she went.

As she ran, Avon checked out the many doors in the hallway. One clearly led to the galley, from the noxious scents that tickled Avon's nose as she passed, while another one sounded like a sparring room or some such, the sounds of people yelling causing Avon to keep moving.

This ship was bigger than she'd expected from the

miniscule cargo hold, but then she saw it: the telltale wiring of a shipboard comm unit. The ship was an older model, so Avon was hoping that the internal comm unit ran through the external comms, an old shipbuilder's cost-saving trick. By powering both sets of comms with a single power source and a single network switch, anyone within the ship could use the external comms, a time-saving feature in case of danger.

Meaning that Avon was heading in the right direction.

Avon skidded around the corner, not paying attention to anything but the exposed comm wiring as she ran. All she needed was a single node, one point of communication. Pain bloomed in her side, and still she kept going, ignoring the stitch. If she was going to make a call for help, she was going to have to push herself. She might not be used to running, but she could figure it out. The human body was meant for such things, even if Avon's body felt like it hated every moment of the physical exertion.

Avon saw the cockpit a little ways up ahead, and hope exploded in her chest. There would definitely be a comm unit there. Good planning, better execution, and she was about to accomplish her goal.

That was when someone grabbed her by the collar of her jacket, hefting her easily off the ground.

"Uh-oh. Looks like someone lost a pup," said someone with a cool voice. Avon was turned around to look right into the face of a woman who seemed vaguely familiar: green skin worked through with silver lines, a long sinuous body, and a serpentine face with a smattering of scales and high cheekbones. The woman reminded Avon of Professor Kip, only instead of wearing a turban, this woman had a crest of rainbow feathers atop her head.

"Where do you think you're going?" the woman asked with a terrifying smile, her teeth pointed razor-sharp. Those were teeth that were meant to rend and tear. Never a good sign.

"I was, um, heading to inspect the engines?" Avon offered with a grin. "I heard a knocking sound. Could be the sublight regulator, and the last thing you want during a haul is for one of those to go out."

"Funny," the woman said, setting Avon back on her feet. "But that's the cockpit. Where there is a comm unit. The engines are on the opposite end of the ship. I'm guessing you know that?" At Avon's sheepish grin the woman jerked her chin back the way Avon had come. "Walk. We're going to pay a visit to Kara Xoo. She'll know what to do with you."

Avon swallowed dryly and began to walk, one foot after another. Drat. This was definitely no good. Not only hadn't she called for help, but this was going to lower her rate of shenanigan success four, maybe five percentage points.

The woman didn't have a blaster, but she didn't need one. Avon was smart. She knew that anyone who could lift her with one arm was not to be messed with, so she walked before the woman, away from the cockpit and back toward the galley with its noxious odors.

The trip back the way Avon had come was much slower, and she had the chance to take in the ship a bit more. It wasn't much. The walls had been stripped bare at some point, the interior wiring exposed and crackling dangerously.

"What happened to your interior walls?" Avon said. "Do you know how much radioactivity your latent thrust return emits when you have the wiring exposed like that? Are you seriously jumping through hyperspace with all of this hanging out?"

"Pup, you don't seem like you're making great choices right about now. Do you even know who we are?" The woman seemed both amused and interested in what Avon had said, and the girl shrugged.

"If you wanted me dead you would've killed me on Haileap." Even in that moment, when she knew she should be panicking, Avon couldn't put aside logic. It was the one thing that had never let her down. "But seriously, who is your ship engineer? Because they are woefully inadequate."

The woman snorted and shook her head. Her hand was suddenly on Avon's shoulder, her skin cold even through the material of Avon's shirt. "This is our door."

The woman stopped in front of the room with all the yelling, and fear washed over Avon. She'd tried to keep the emotion at bay, but with the unknown looming large, she found that she was suddenly reluctant to take a single step forward into the melee beyond.

When the door swished open Avon realized she had miscalculated. She'd thought they were on a smaller Nihil ship, one of those belonging to the Strikes, as they were called. After the tragedy on Wevo, Avon had fallen into a wormhole of Nihil facts and lore, pulling everything she could from the holonet. She'd learned about the Nihil, how they worked, and their structure. She was certain most of what she read was wrong. One source seemed to think that the Nihil had built a gravity well projector in the Berenge sector, a feat so impossible that Avon had read the article out loud to a completely disinterested J-6, stifling laughter the entire time.

But the one thing everyone agreed on was the Nihil structure: Strikes were the smallest group, then the larger Clouds, with Tempests being the largest and most dangerous, second only to the Storm, a gathering of all the Nihil.

From what Avon could tell from the crush of bodies in the room they entered, this was far bigger than a Strike. This was big trouble.

And she was smack-dab in the middle of it all.

Imri looked at the destroyed noodle cart and sighed before holding his hand out and moving it so the cart was turned right side up. What could the Nihil have possibly gotten out of destroying a noodle cart? And not just any noodle cart, but the best one in all of Port Haileap? Koko Noodle had made the spiciest, tangiest noodles, and now Koko was nowhere to be found and the cart itself was little more than a bunch of twisted metal.

A Jedi was not supposed to nurture negative feelings, but Imri really hoped whoever had destroyed the noodle

cart ended up with burrs in their underthings. It was the least they deserved.

Imri frowned as he used the Force to straighten out a few of the dents in the noodle cart, so that by the time he was done it looked more or less the way he remembered it. Once that was complete he turned his attention to the next bit of debris.

"Imri," Vernestra called, and he turned to see his master walking toward him. He couldn't help smiling. If anyone had told him that he would one day be on his way to being a Jedi Knight, and that a prodigy like Vernestra Rwoh was going to be the one to help him get there, he would've thought they were teasing him. She moved through the space with such calm and self-assurance, and Imri always felt a little better when she was around, her inner stillness settling some of Imri's perpetual worry.

But at her approach Imri caught the sharp edge of Vernestra's concern, and he frowned. "What's wrong? Where's Avon?"

"The Nihil have taken her, and we are going to get her back and teach them a very valuable lesson about theft!"

J-6 said, stomping forward before Vernestra could speak. "Good to see you again, Imri. Do you still want to kill some Nihil?"

Embarrassment surged through Imri, and his cheeks flushed as he laughed nervously. The droid, who had at some point been on the receiving end of Avon's tinkering, was like no other droid he'd ever met before.

"No, I don't want to kill anyone, Jay-Six. But what do you mean the Nihil took her?" Imri was confused. Why would the Nihil kidnap Avon? Unless . . . "Do you think they know who she is?"

Vernestra shook her head. "I don't know. Let's talk to Master Jorinda and see what she knows."

"We have to find her, Vern. Avon is our friend." Imri could feel panic beginning to rise, and he took a deep breath and let it out to try to control it.

Vernestra put a calming hand on Imri's shoulder. "We'll find her."

Imri nodded, and the trio—with J-6 clanking along and muttering idle threats as they walked—found Master Jorinda quite quickly. She was standing near a crew of droids who were very carefully moving debris and sweeping up broken glass from a row of storefronts that had been looted, their contents stolen by the Nihil.

"Jedi Vernestra! Did you find your friend?"

Vernestra shook her head. Imri watched as J-6 approached the group of droids, explaining to them how best to clean up the mess. Tears pricked his eyes at the destruction. How terrible it had to be for people, in a moment of violence, to lose everything they'd worked so hard for.

Imri tried to remind himself they were just things, and that the Force worked as it would. Perhaps this loss would lead the citizens of Haileap to rebuild bigger and better. Still, it was hard to look at the violence wrought by the Nihil and think it had anything to do with the Force. Balance in all things was important, but where did cruelty fit into that structure? Nowhere, as far as he was concerned.

"Master Jorinda," Vernestra said, inclining her head as a sign of respect. "I know you have a lot to do, but Avon Starros, daughter of Senator Ghirra Starros of Hosnian Prime, seems to be missing. One of her friends said that the Nihil took her."

"Oh, I know Avon," Master Jorinda said, "and the Nihil kidnapping someone is terrible. The Nihil are getting desperate, and with nowhere to run it seems like they're turning to even worse tactics than before. Administrator Rico!" the Jedi called, and a rotund Gran wearing the distinct uniform of the Republic hurried over, his three eye stalks waving in agitation.

"Master Jorinda," he said, bowing.

"Did you finish the head count? These Jedi say that we're missing Avon Starros."

"Ah, not yet. We have been tending to the dead," Rico said, the floppy ears on the sides of his head drooping sadly.

Master Jorinda nodded. "Understandable. Please have one of the droids account for everyone. We know we're missing one person. Let's see if there's anyone else."

The administrator moved away, and Master Jorinda sighed. "I'm afraid we are woefully unprepared for any of this. They hit us so quickly that we barely had time to even muster a response. We've been lax since the Republic Coalition forces departed Haileap." She shook her head sadly. "We thought the problem was handled, to be honest. When those ships appeared it wasn't until they began firing upon us that we realized they weren't just the usual travelers passing through."

Vernestra nodded in understanding, but Imri wanted to stomp his foot in frustration. He couldn't believe how calm Vernestra was being. Who knew what the Nihil were doing to Avon! They would most likely torture her and then ransom her back to the Republic. They had to save her as quickly as possible.

But they had to find her first.

"Do you think Master Maru would know where they went?" Imri asked suddenly.

Vernestra frowned. "What are you thinking?"

"Well, the Nihil don't usually just strike once, right? They like to raid a few places at a time before they leave a sector. At least, that's what they used to do before they had Jedi to worry about. Maybe there were some other attacks and we can figure out where they're headed based on that?"

"Good idea," Master Jorinda said with a nod. "I wish I could be more help, but we need to finish cleaning up Port Haileap and take care of the victims here. And tend to our dead." Master Jorinda's voice cracked a little bit at that, and Imri recalled that she'd lost a Jedi. Avon might be missing, but there were a lot of people on Haileap that were hurting right now, including Master Jorinda.

"The people here . . . it will be hard for us to continue, to rebuild," Master Jorinda said when she'd finally wrestled her sadness back under control. "I will send a message to the Council as well as Starlight so that we can alert the frontier that the Nihil seem to be taking hostages. And we will also determine if anyone else was taken."

"Should we stay and help with the cleanup?" Imri wondered aloud.

Vernestra shook her head. "We have to find Avon. And quickly, before anything happens to her."

"Yes. I hope you find your friend," Master Jorinda said with a sad expression.

"Let us know if you hear anything, including whether any others are missing. It seems strange that the Nihil would suddenly get involved in kidnapping people at this point. Just . . . it's not like them," Vernestra said with a frown. Waves of confusion and worry surrounded her, and Imri had to focus to make sure the feelings didn't become his own. He liked knowing how his master was feeling. He often knew when he'd done something right without her saying a word, because he could feel the approval coming from her, like smelling a dish of something delicious.

But when the feelings were sad or troubling, Imri had to work to keep from being overwhelmed by them. Too much sadness and fear could bury even the strongest Jedi, and Imri was just a Padawan. He had to be patient with his limited abilities, and that came with pacing himself.

So he held himself very carefully as they returned to the ship to call Master Maru, trying not to let Vernestra's worry mingle with his own and become something unmanageable. It wasn't until they had almost reached their vessel that Imri realized J-6 was following them like a metallic shadow.

"Jay-Six, what are you doing?" Imri asked.

"I'm coming along, obviously. Those Nihil scum took my charge! Plus, Avon promised me a galactic map update. Some of my routes are decades out of date."

Vernestra frowned at the droid. "Why do you need updated galactic maps?"

"In case I decide to travel," the droid said. "I've heard the Naboo Lake Country is stunning, and I think I'd like to scan the landscape for myself."

Imri and Vernestra exchanged looks. Avon had definitely been tinkering with the droid again.

The realization just made Imri miss the girl even more. Once they found her, he was going to listen to all her stories, even the ones that confused him with their scientific complexity.

They climbed aboard the *Wishful Thinking*, and Vernestra used the comm unit to call Maru while Imri launched the ship, ascending into the sky and away from Port Haileap.

"We've had five reports of the Nihil attacking over the past three hours," Master Maru said through the comm unit in response to Vernestra's query. "One on Hon-Tallos, one on Thelj, and another at an outpost near Tiikae."

"Anyone gone missing from those attacks?" Vernestra asked.

"Not on the outpost or Hon-Tallos, but here's something that might prove useful . . . the Jedi on Dalna are saying that it seems like people are disappearing in the outlying towns around Saludad, the capital city. But from the reports it seems like they're still investigating the matter. What's this about? Are you assisting Master Jorinda with the cleanup on Haileap?"

"I heard a call for help, and Avon Starros is missing. We think the Nihil took her, but we aren't sure if they know who she is. I think this might be tied to something bigger, Master Maru," Vernestra said, her green face twisted in contemplation.

"There is also the chance that she went with them herself," said J-6, behind Imri. "She has been known to do sillier things in the pursuit of knowledge."

"Ahhh," Master Maru said, the silence heavy as he thought. "We should send a message to her mother on Coruscant. The senator will want to know her daughter is missing."

"She may have gotten a ransom demand if the Nihil know who Avon is," Imri said.

"That's true," Maru said. "I'll let Master Nubarron know that you're going to be using the shuttle for an extended period of time, and will inform Marshal Kriss of the situation, as well. Do what you can to find Avon Starros. If the Nihil are kidnapping people and taking hostages now, we'll need to get that information out."

"We aren't sure that's what's happening just yet," Vernestra said. "But we'll check back in with you once we have more information. For now we're going to head toward Dalna, since that's closest."

They signed off, and Vernestra sat back as Imri flew the shuttle out of the range of Haileap's planetary gravity shadow to make the jump to hyperspace. Imri cleared his throat.

"Do you think if you, um, maybe meditate with Avon in mind, you could find her?" he asked. He'd learned recently that Vernestra had the ability to sometimes see other places in the galaxy if she fell into a hypnotic state while in hyperspace. It wasn't something she liked to do on purpose. Vernestra preferred to let the Force guide her rather than directing her efforts, but with Avon missing, this seemed like a good time to be a little more proactive with her abilities.

"I will. Let's head to Dalna, though. The temple there has a number of Jedi, and we're going to need help."

Imri nodded and bit his lip. How many Nihil could be left? Hadn't the Jedi and the Republic already taken care of the threat?

Imri did not want to consider just what kind of danger they were headed into.

Avon would not let them see how scared she was. The Nihil stared at her, a few of them hooting and hollering as she entered. There were species of every kind: humans, Ithorians, Devaronians, a few Soikans, and even a Wookiee, their long braid hanging low and threaded through with beads. But none of them looked quite as fierce or terrifying as the Quarren sitting on what could only be called a throne in the middle of the room.

"Deva. Did you find yourself a new pet?" the Quarren woman asked, smiling, her pointed teeth crooked and jagged. Avon knew that Quarrens didn't eat humans, but that didn't stop Avon's heart from pounding and her palms from slicking with sweat.

Fight-or-flight response, she reminded herself. *All of this is because I'm scared, not because I'm in danger.*

That wasn't entirely true, though. She was far from home on a ship full of Nihil, all of them looking at her like she was a piping hot plate of bocha, all flaky and delicious.

Avon was in a lot of danger. No one would have faulted her for panicking.

"One of your recruits was out wandering the hallway. On her way to the cockpit, to be exact," the reptilian woman said, crossing her arms with a shrug. "I'm guessing Bobert had dinner duty again?"

"They jumped me," the Trandoshan with the yellow eyes said, sounding upset. "I was trying to feed the mites, and they all attacked me like a band of feral ronks!"

"You kidnapped us. What do you expect?" Avon demanded. As soon as she spoke she regretted the outburst, and she tried to duck her head and disappear as soon as the words were out of her mouth.

"Ahhh. Spunky," the woman on the throne said. She stood and walked toward Avon. There were dozens of scars all over her body, all of them dyed blue. The woman reminded Avon of Gwishi, one of the Nihil who had destroyed the *Steady Wing*, killing Jedi Master Douglas Sunvale. Avon had liked the laid-back Master Douglas, and she tried to summon his memory to give her strength.

The Nihil were bad and scary, but more important, the things they did had hurt people Avon cared about. She'd do well to remember that.

"What is your name?" the Quarren woman asked, her face tentacles dancing as though they were sniffing at Avon. She was glad she'd taken a shower that morning.

"Avon . . . Sunvale," she said, crossing her arms. Avon didn't know how much the Nihil kept up with politics, but Starros was a powerful name in the Core, and it wouldn't do to let the woman know that Avon came from such a family.

"Avon. Good name. I am Kara Xoo. Welcome to my Tempest." Kara Xoo raised her hands to indicate the people surrounding them, and the Nihil in the room hooted and hollered in response, thumping their chests in a way that would've scared Avon if she hadn't already been beyond such things. Avon was learning that there was a point where you became so scared that you couldn't feel your body anymore, and she was currently in that place. The tips of her fingers were cold, but other than that she couldn't sense anything about herself. She felt as though she was watching the exchange from far away, the moment happening to someone else.

"If we're part of your Tempest, why are we locked up? Without so much as a refresher?" Avon said, her bravado giving her words an edge. There would be a price to pay for this display. Avon was sure of it. She'd dealt with bullies like the Nihil before. They might be nice to you for a moment, but it never lasted. And when their amusement faded, that's when the hitting started.

But Kara Xoo smiled, flashing those pointed teeth. "That is for your safety. And you might join my Tempest, but not quite yet, hatchling. You must earn a spot with my Nihil. Deva, take her back to the others. And make sure the door is secured."

An arm wrapped around Avon's waist, and she flailed as she was taken from the room.

The trip from Kara Xoo's throne room to the cargo hold where she'd started out was shorter than Avon had thought. Deva dumped her on the floor and then exited without a word, and Avon sat up with a groan as the other kids gathered around.

"Did you send a message to the Jedi?" Petri asked.

Avon shook her head. "I found the cockpit, but that woman caught me before I could do anything."

"What was she?" asked Liam, and Krylind smacked him lightly.

"That's rude. You aren't supposed to ask people that."

"So, you didn't get a hold of the Jedi," Petri said, crossing his arms. "And now they think we were trying to escape. What if they decide not to feed us? Or throw us out of a hatch into space?"

"Or sell us to the Zygerrians?" Krylind said, her bottom lip trembling.

"They aren't going to do any of that," Avon said, her brain replaying the previous few moments, analyzing them with a cool, scientific perspective. "I think they're going to make us Nihil."

CHAPTER EIGHT

Vernestra took a deep breath and let it out, trying to meditate. She could feel the nervous energy coming from Imri as he watched her, hoping that somehow, some way her ability to see other parts of the galaxy while she was in hyperspace would lead them to Avon. Vernestra wanted the same thing. She was worried, more than she was letting on to Imri. The Nihil were killers and scoundrels. If they'd taken Avon there was nothing good that could come of it.

But Vernestra didn't have time for all those worries and wayward thoughts. If she wanted to find Avon she had to focus, on sensing the girl and figuring out just what had become of her.

Vernestra took another deep breath, letting it out slowly. She imagined herself as a small, burbling brook, babbling and twisting across a peaceful landscape, flowing into a stream and then a river, a wide, vast body of water that grew and grew until it was an ocean of possibility— cool, blue, refreshing. This was how Vernestra perceived the Force. While the Force was not a truly physical thing, but more a field of energy linking all living things, it was most helpful for Vernestra to visualize it as water. Water flowed and twisted; it conformed to its container and sometimes changed its form altogether. If Vernestra wanted to find Avon, she needed to do so through the Force.

The Force would know where Avon was. Now, whether Vernestra would be able to find a single brown-skinned human girl within the mass of all the living things in the galaxy was the real question.

Vernestra was floating within the Force, drifting, when she heard a voice. It sounded like Avon's, but Vernestra didn't want to break the connection by trying too hard. Sometimes reaching for the Force was the worst thing one could do. It was in those moments that a Jedi could lose their connection, focusing too much on the problems of their physical form and not enough on letting the Force do as it pleased. The living Force might be one of action and movement, but it was the cosmic Force that Vernestra strained toward now. The vast consciousness would know where Avon had got to, and whether or not she was safe.

"Avon . . . Sunvale."

"Kara Xoo."

There was a slight bump, and Vernestra was jolted out of the vision. She hadn't seen anything, but she had heard Avon! She'd know her voice anywhere. It wasn't what Vernestra had been aiming for, but it was better than flying around the galaxy hoping they were heading in the right direction.

"Vern, did you see something?" Imri asked, glancing over at her. "You seem . . . not exactly happy, but hopeful, maybe?"

"I didn't see anything, but I heard something. Avon was talking to someone. I don't know where she was, but I heard her say her name was Avon Sunvale."

"Sunvale . . ." Imri's voice trailed off, a sad, wistful

smile on his face. "She used Master Doug's name to avoid giving herself away. Smart."

"There was another phrase. Kara Xoo. I think it was a name, but I didn't recognize the voice."

"Do you think it was a Nihil?"

"Yes, but the question is, how long ago was it?" One of the problems with Vernestra's hyperspace visions was that they were unpredictable, and not just in how often they appeared but in when the events were happening. She was never sure if they were occurring when she saw them or before she saw them, or if she was seeing things that had already happened. It was very confusing, and Vernestra pinched the bridge of her nose as a headache bloomed behind her eyes.

"While you were out I called the temple on Dalna. I hope that was okay," Imri said with a sheepish grin.

"Oh, good thinking." Vernestra realized that she was so worried about Avon she'd completely neglected connecting with the Jedi on Dalna. She took another deep breath and let it out. Just because she was concerned for a friend didn't mean she could toss aside all her responsibilities as a Jedi. "What did they say?"

"They were actually really glad we'd reached out. Apparently there's been some . . . difficulty, they said, in working with the local government. They didn't want to say too much over the comm, so we're supposed to meet them as soon as we land."

Vernestra's belly gurgled and she groaned. "Over food, I hope. Those ration packs never keep me full."

"I know. I really hope Dalna has something like the spicy noodles from Port Haileap." Imri sighed. "Poor noodle cart."

"I would like a liter of joba oil, if anyone cares," came the droid's voice from the rear of the shuttle. Vernestra had almost forgotten that J-6 had come along with them, and she tried not to sigh as she twisted around in her seat to look at the droid. "But if you don't mind, I think I will remain on the ship and charge myself. I'm feeling a bit run-down since Avon disappeared, and maybe that will put things to rights. But bring me back a joba oil."

"We'll see what we can do."

Imri landed the shuttle gently in the docking area near Dalna's Jedi temple. The building was small but beautiful. Strange orange and white flowers lined the walkway on either side of the path, and a brook flowed with bril-liant cerulean water not too far away, a radiant red moss growing on the rocks nearest the water. Dalna had a small temperate zone and two polar zones, and even though it was a very tiny planet, it had joined the Republic to much fanfare due to its production of gnostra berries, which were known throughout the galaxy for creating a particularly delightful wine. Vernestra had never tasted it, but she knew it fetched a fair price at market.

The Jedi temple on Dalna was newer, only a century and a half old. It had been built in the aftermath of a devastating battle on the planet, and even though Dalna was relatively close to Port Haileap, all things considered, Vernestra had never had a chance to visit the temple. She found that even though it was rather modest compared with the Temple on Coruscant, it gave her the same sense of peace.

"Oh, oh! Are those . . . tookas?" Imri exclaimed as he disembarked behind Vernestra, J-6 left on the shuttle, plugged into a port.

The entrance to the temple was crowded with tooka cats in varying shades: a gray one, a violet one, and a deep green one that yawned as they approached, showing its teeth. Imri held his hand out to the nearest one, and it let out a growly sound and wove between his legs.

"Why don't we have any tookas on Starlight? It seems like they'd be better than the maintenance droids at clearing out pests," Imri said as he scratched the animal behind its ears.

"Probably because someone has to pick up all the poop, and maintenance droids are funny when it comes to that sort of thing." A wizened Twi'lek with yellow skin and wrinkly lekku exited the temple, a smile on her face. "I'm Master Nyla Quinn. You must be Imri."

"Yes, Master Quinn. This is my master, Jedi Knight Vernestra Rwoh," he said with a grin. "Thanks for helping us out."

"Oh, no problem. But like I said when you called, I'm not sure how much help we can be. We're a ways from the city, and for the most part we're more of a meditation temple than anything close to what you see on Starlight Beacon. Yacek and Lyssa, the Jedi Knights here with me, went into the city to pick up supplies. We'll eat the evening meal when they return. I hope you're all hungry."

"Starving," Vernestra said with a grin, which faded into a frown. "It's good to meet you, Master Quinn. But Master Maru said that you have had some people go missing in the past few weeks. Shouldn't we see to the issue of the missing Dalnans before we eat?"

"Nyla, please. And I'm afraid the matter is not so clearcut, more speculation on our part than anything else. I think you'll understand better once I explain. Come on in here before Rascal there decides to take a nibble of your Padawan's braid," she said, gesturing to where Imri stood cradling one of the tookas like a baby, cooing to the animal. "They seem cute and cuddly, but they have a mean streak a kilometer wide."

"That's what makes them so great," Imri said with another grin. "They are just as nature made them."

It wasn't hot outside, but Vernestra appreciated the coolness of the temple. The stone floor was swept clean, and she noted a small library with a comm unit and a terminal and three chairs. Most of the rooms were empty, a bedroll tucked off to one side, waiting for a Jedi who needed the time and space to meditate. Temples like the one on Dalna were places where Jedi sometimes went to recover from difficult events. After the tragedy on Valo, Vernestra had toyed with the idea of taking some time to do such a thing, but her commitment to Imri hadn't allowed her to go away and commune with the Force. Now she thought maybe once they got Avon back, it would be a good lesson for them, to come here for a week or two and practice being one with the Force.

But thinking about Avon brought her back to the reason they were there, and when they had sat at a long table in the communal area, she cleared her throat.

"Master Nyla. About the possibility of people going missing here on Dalna?"

The old Twi'lek woman leaned back with a sigh. "That's all we know, as well. It seems like a few of the families on the smaller homesteads have left, but whether it was by choice or not, we have no idea. We've made inquiries, but they've been pushed aside time and again, and it isn't our place to intervene unless there is a formal request for help."

"Why wouldn't the Dalnans want your help if people are missing?" Imri asked.

Master Nyla's face twisted into a pensive frown. "We aren't exactly best friends with the Dalnans. Even after joining the Republic, they still are very standoffish. Not much for strangers. They tolerate us all right, will even work with us, but some time before this temple was built, there was a tragedy and they've blamed the Jedi ever since. And we try to respect that. There was some talk of closing the temple a few years back since we didn't seem to be welcome, but the Dalnans resisted. They like having us here, but also appreciate us keeping our distance, so we try to respect that, too. Yacek had asked about some ships he saw out on the horizon while out for a hike, especially when a couple of the families who would sometimes visit the temple for medical help disappeared. The local city administrator said they hadn't had any reports of problems, but nothing more. And when Yacek tried to push, the response was quite curt." Master Nyla shook her head. "Like I said, we pretty much keep to ourselves since that's how the Dalnans like it."

"So you don't think the Nihil are involved?" Vernestra asked. She'd hoped that finding Avon would be easy, but this was turning out to be a dead end.

"I couldn't say, but Dalna has been left to its own devices while the Nihil have terrorized the rest of the frontier. Why are you so interested in the Nihil? In another week or two they'll be completely finished. I heard the Starlight Jedi were going after that Eye of theirs, Lourna Dee." Master Nyla's face took on a look of disgust. "To think another Twi'lek was behind so much of this pain and destruction, and the loss of Master Loden Greatstorm, one of the finest Jedi I ever met. The sooner they can bring her to justice, the better." The older Jedi shook her head just as someone called out a greeting from the back of the temple, distracting the Jedi from their conversation.

A small human woman with pale skin and long auburn hair, and a human man, strapping and big like Imri but with warm golden skin and long, straight black hair to the middle of his back, walked into the temple carrying woven bags full of fruits and other things. The tookas immediately flocked to the man, yowling piteously, and he laughed, the sound echoing off the stone walls of the temple.

"Someone smells the moon fish I bought. Welcome, Jedi! I am Yacek Sparkburn. Welcome to our humble temple."

"And I'm Lyssa Votz, the archivist here." She smiled

warmly at Vernestra and Imri. "Let us know if there's anything we can do to help you during your stay."

Yacek set the bags on the table and began to dig through them. "It's going to take me some time to prepare something, so enjoy these while you wait. I could hear your bellies grumbling when I walked in." The man handed Imri and Vernestra each a round, purple fruit that was so big they had to hold it with both hands. "That's a durga berry. It looks big, but it's mostly juice, so be careful when you bite into it."

"What he means to say is, those berries have ruined many a tabard," Lyssa said with a laugh. "I don't know why we keep getting them."

"Because they are delicious. Also, you can only find them on Dalna. They can't even export them, they spoil so quickly," Yacek said with a shrug. "Enjoy!"

"Thank you," Vernestra said, waiting to watch Imri attack the thing before she tried it herself. They didn't have a change of clothing, and Vernestra was loath to get purple juice all over the front of her clothes. "I'm Vernestra Rwoh, and this is my Padawan, Imri Cantaros."

"They get younger all the time, eh, Nyla?" Yacek said, tossing the older woman a berry of her own. He offered one to Lyssa and she politely declined, moving off deeper into the temple to attend to her own duties.

"Sparkburn," Imri said, also eyeing his berry before biting into it. He looked at Vernestra, and they both watched as Nyla took a delicate bite from the top before tilting the fruit back to drink the juice. "Are you any relation to Jordanna Sparkburn? She used to be the San Tekka deputy on Tiikae."

"Couldn't say," Yacek said, scratching his head. "There's a lot of us Sparkburns, and before I went to the temple, my family did live in a San Tekka compound. I think the saying I've heard around the galaxy is that every San Tekka was a Sparkburn, but not every Sparkburn was a San Tekka. Or was it the other way around?" He shrugged before picking up his bags once more. "Anyway, I'm going to go prepare something to eat. See you all in an hour or so."

"Back to the Nihil," Vernestra said, unable to let the matter go. "You haven't seen them here, so where do you think the missing people have gone? If they are indeed missing?"

"We don't know, but I'm hoping you can help us. Since you and your Padawan have experience against the Nihil and the Drengir, you might be able to help us get some answers out of the government or at least find something we've overlooked. I know you traveled some time ago with the ambassadors aboard the *Steady Wing*. I believe the Dalnans are hiding something, and perhaps your history with them can help soften their resistance. If nothing else, you and your Padawan can add a fresh perspective to the matter. Please at least help put our concerns to rest before you leave."

Vernestra did not sigh, but she wanted to. She didn't want to stay on Dalna if this was a dead end. She wanted to figure out where the Nihil had taken Avon.

But putting aside the possible danger on Dalna to go looking for Avon when they had no clue as to where she might be was irresponsible and dangerously close to defying the overall guidance of the Order. A Jedi was supposed to protect life equally and to the best of their ability, and that did not mean friends or the children of Republic officials got special treatment.

Besides, if something bad was happening on Dalna, it

could somehow tie back to the Nihil. They were turning out to have their thieving fingers in more matters throughout the galaxy than anyone had ever imagined. And even if it wasn't the Nihil, the Dalnans deserved the Jedi's assistance. Vernestra would be remiss to leave the matter on Dalna unfinished.

Sometimes the hardest thing to do was the right thing.

"Of course, Master Nyla. We'll help you investigate this matter and put everyone's concerns to rest before we continue our search for Avon." Vernestra just hoped that wouldn't take too long.

"Thank you. We appreciate it. Why don't you two get some rest while Yacek makes the food?" Nyla said, standing with a sigh. "We have a nice meditation garden out back near the brook if you'd like to collect yourselves. Or if you want to look through the archives, Lyssa can help with that. We keep a log of all the reports and there might be something I've forgotten. I'll call the administrator's office in Saludad and see if they can fit us in tomorrow. It might not look like it, but night comes on quick here, and it gets very cold. It's dangerous to go wandering about while the ice gators are out. They leave the polar ice caps and come into the temperate zone this time of year, so it'll be safer to talk to the administrator in the morning."

Since they were obligated to help the Dalna Jedi, Vernestra decided she would sit with Lyssa and see if there was anything in the databank about children going missing after Nihil attacks, and then let that information drive her next steps. If they wanted to find Avon, they were going to have to be smart about things. Still, she felt agitated and anxious. It wasn't at all like her, and Vernestra realized she was really worried. Avon was a smart girl, but that was the problem. The right person could take a smart kid like Avon and find ways to make her do terrible things, whether she realized it or not.

Vernestra finally took a bite of the durga fruit, which immediately splashed a bit of bright purple juice on her tabard. She sighed just as Imri exclaimed, the front of his tabard covered in the brilliant juice.

"I'll also rustle you up a change of clothing," Master Nyla said with a knowing smile, and Vernestra gave in and devoured the fruit, trying not to worry quite so much about making a mess.

It was absolutely delicious.

Avon poked at the bowl of joppa stew their minder had dropped off, and tried to force herself to eat. It was the first rule of being kidnapped. You ate what they offered, drank what they offered, and used the facilities whenever possible. It seemed like a terrible idea—what if the food was poisoned?—but people who kidnapped you usually didn't try to keep you alive only to kill you before they'd gotten what they wanted.

It was the kind of terrible thing a person learned when their mother was a senator.

Avon had been kidnapped before, but this time felt

different. An hour or so after her escape, the strange woman with the rainbow feather crest returned, this time with a box of holo games.

"Some of these are broken, but bored pups are dangerous pups," she said, dropping the crate in the middle of the room. Avon had half a mind to charge the woman, try to overpower her, but then she remembered how easily the Nihil had picked her up and brought her back to the cargo hold, so she stayed where she was, waiting until the door slid closed before abandoning the cold stew and checking out the contents of the box.

"Ugh, these are rubbish," Petri said, his voice full of disgust. "*Sky Command*? This game is like, a century old."

"Let me see that," Avon said, her heart soaring as she examined the contents of the box. Petri was right; most of the games were trash and completely unplayable. But that wasn't a problem for Avon. The components in the games were exactly what she needed.

"What are you doing with that?" Krylind said as Avon slammed one of the games into the metal floor of the cargo hold, breaking the plasticene case open a tiny bit.

"Did you know the components within a game system

are almost identical to a basic door lock system?" she said, pulling a few wires loose.

"Wait, are you going to try to slice the door lock?" Petri asked, leaning over her shoulder as she began to examine the pieces, putting them into three piles: useful, maybe useful, and trash. A few of the diodes and circuit boards were fried, the black scorch marks making their uselessness clear, but most of the parts were just fine. It had always fascinated and frustrated Avon that a single broken piece in a system could bring down the entire device, but in that moment she was thankful.

"I'm not going to *try* and slice the door lock. I'm going to slice the door lock. That mechanism is a Stebbish Series Y, which is at least a century old, if not two." Avon had tried not to think too hard about the age of the ship when she'd been running through the hallways, but now that she was back in the cargo hold, she kept wondering how it was that the Nihil had gotten their hands on such an old trawler. And she mostly tried not to think about the likelihood that the ship's life-support systems would fail utterly and kill them all. Working on a plan for escape was a great distraction. "It shouldn't be all that hard to slice it with what we have here. I'll build a connector, try to get out and call for help."

Krylind crossed her arms and shook her head. "Maybe you should just leave it alone. The Trandoshan roared at us last time, and you're lucky the Shani didn't kill you when she brought you back."

That made Avon pause. "Shani? What's that?" She'd never heard the name before, and Avon prided herself on being well-informed.

"The woman with the feathered crest. I've only seen a few of them, since they usually stay on the edges of the frontier. They're dangerous, and I heard they can swallow people whole."

"That's silly," Avon said, immediately dismissing the other girl. "I think my mentor is the same species and she's never eaten a single person."

"Maybe you just weren't there when she did," Petri said.

"Or maybe people, even those from the same place, all have different ideas and values," Avon muttered.

"You're weird," Petri said.

Avon ignored the boy and returned to her work. The other kids all went off to the side to confer among themselves, deciding something. Avon didn't care what they discussed. She was focused on connecting wires the best she could without a proper tool kit.

Time passed, and when Avon looked up, the other kids had all huddled up with blankets and were fast asleep. Her eyes were gritty, and she bit back yet another yawn, but Avon refused to give up. She knew that Vernestra and Imri were looking for her. She could feel it. There was no way they would hear about the attack on Port Haileap and not make sure she was okay, and when they found her gone they would definitely come looking for her. She would do everything she could to get them a message.

Finally, her slicer was ready. It wasn't much to look at, a piece of circuit board and a bunch of odds and ends, but it didn't have to be impressive for such an old lock. An astromech could have easily sliced the thing if there had been a droid willing to help. A sharp pain of longing stabbed Avon, and she blinked away hot tears. She missed J-6. If she'd been there, no one would have messed with Avon. The thought was too close to sadness, so she took a deep breath and blew it away.

Focus on the task at hand, Starros, Avon thought.

She hooked her cobbled-together slicer into the control panel and waited while the board sequenced the lock. After less than a minute, there was a click as the door released and then slid open.

Avon stood with a triumphant smile and stepped out into the hallway—only to see the Shani woman, Deva, leaning against one of the few intact portions of the wall.

"I thought you would've been out a few minutes earlier, but I get it. It's late and you've had a long day."

Avon swallowed dryly, her heart pounding. She knew that very few humans died from fear, but all she could think of was what Krylind had said about the Shani swallowing people whole.

"Are you going to eat me?" Avon asked.

The woman didn't seem surprised by the question. "No. I have a job for you."

Deva jerked her head at Avon, and the girl followed the woman through the corridors of the ship. Avon tried to remember the directions of how many twists and turns they took, but she got the feeling they'd passed certain places more than once, a purposeful move so she wouldn't be able to find her way later even if she tried.

A door slid open and an old Siniteen stood on the other side. His cranium was overly large to accommodate his brain, and Avon was entranced and horrified by the veins that pulsed in his temples. "Not now, Deva. I'm busy."

"Stop complaining, Royce. This is Avon Sunvale. She's smart, and she just sliced the door lock with the random bits from a few broken game systems."

"So, what does she know about sublight engines and Path drives? Or calculating jumps?"

Avon shook her head. "I can't calculate jumps in my head, but I've rebuilt several sublight engines and repivoted a hyperdrive a time or two. How do your Path engines differ from a traditional hyperdrive, other than being external so you can give everyone a nice green target to aim at?"

The Siniteen watched Avon with beady eyes for a moment before he laughed. "Heh. I said the same thing, but I'm surrounded by fools and they ignored me. All right, let's see what you can do."

"Be good, pup," Deva said, showing Avon her teeth. "If you aren't, I'll eat you."

Avon was only half sure she was kidding.

When Imri woke, his first thought was of Avon. He'd dreamed of her, not a Jedi vision but a memory of one of their last times together with Jedi Master Douglas Sunvale. They'd been out in the big marblewood forest that covered most of Haileap. Master Douglas had been teaching them about the local plants and animals, explaining how each one used the habitat to its advantage. Imri hadn't been very interested, but Avon had been enthralled, and when Imri had nearly stepped on a flowering snake, Avon had been the one to grab him and point out the creature nestled amid a patch of wildflowers.

"Step carefully," she'd said, smiling at Imri, her curls wild and her eyes bright. "Remember what Master Douglas said: 'It's no good to go charging into things you know nothing about.'"

It had been a rare moment from Avon, who was usually the one plunging headlong into situations, and Imri believed that his dreaming of the memory was a warning he should heed. Whether the message was from whatever part of Master Douglas was now within the Force or his own subconscious, Imri didn't know. But he kept the memory close as he left his room and went to break his fast.

Dinner the night before had been delicious. Yacek was an amazing cook, and both he and Master Nyla, the Dalna temple Jedi, were happy to have other Jedi around. They'd discussed some of the adventures Imri and Vernestra had undertaken over the past year, fighting the Drengir and the horror of the Nihil attacking the Republic Fair on Valo. Yacek had been especially interested in their time on Wevo and the Gravity's Heart, the gravity well projector the Nihil had built. As they'd shared their adventures, Imri had found himself feeling more and more overwhelmed.

It had been more than a year of triumphs, but they'd lost so many. And now they were in danger of losing Avon, as well. Imri didn't want to lose any more of his friends. That wasn't attachment, as Vernestra always warned about. That was just being a good person.

Imri didn't want to stay to help the Dalnan Jedi. He wanted to find Avon. Even Vernestra hadn't seemed thrilled about staying on Dalna. But that was one of the hard things about being a Jedi. It was about responsibility, and a Jedi had a duty to help as many people as possible, not just the people they liked.

It didn't make it any easier, though.

Imri had excused himself to go to bed when Master Nyla and Vernestra began to discuss the Jedi working with the Republic, and what the Order's responsibility was to the Republic. It was a conversation that always made Imri deeply uncomfortable. As a Padawan he didn't think he should have an opinion on the matter, but the truth was that he didn't like the idea of so much fighting. Lightsabers should be used only for defense, a principle both Vernestra and Master Douglas had stated repeatedly. But where was the line between defense and offense? And where was the balance between protecting life and taking it because that was the easy thing to do?

Imri didn't know, and every time the conversation came up, more and more since the Jedi had mostly defeated the Nihil, his face grew hot and he had a feeling he could only describe as spiky and disconcerting. He didn't like the way people discussed taking life so freely, but he also didn't know how he felt one way or the other. So it was just easier to avoid the conversation altogether.

In the morning, he was relieved to find that Yacek and Vernestra were waiting for him when he entered the common room. A spread of fruit and cheeses was laid out on the table, along with a hearty loaf of bread. Imri was relieved to see that there were no durga berries today. They were delicious, but Master Nyla had been hard pressed to find a tabard in his size, and he didn't want to tempt disaster by eating another one.

"I was just about to come find you," Vernestra said with a smile, the tattoos outside of the corners of her eyes crinkling.

"Sorry, I think I was more tired from our training

yesterday than I realized. Are we heading into the city today?"

"Yes, Yacek was giving me an overview of the people here and the city of Saludad, and Lyssa is going to prepare some reading for us on the Nihil's activities in this sector over the past few months, just in case there is something we might have overlooked. Don't worry, you didn't miss much."

Imri hurriedly fixed himself a plate and sat down in one of the empty chairs. Immediately one of the tookas jumped into his lap and began to make growly noises, so he broke off a piece of cheese and fed it to the feline, careful to make sure the tooka didn't catch his fingers.

"Gemmy seems to like you," Yacek said with a laugh. "He doesn't like anyone."

"I like him, too," Imri said, scratching the beast behind the ears. For a moment he thought of the handsy he'd befriended on Wevo and his tragic end, but he put the memory to the side and tried to focus on what Yacek was saying.

"Okay, so where was I . . . ? Oh, yes. Saludad is the capital city, but I want you to manage your expectations. It's nothing like what you'd expect from a planetary capital. It's small. In fact, Dalna itself only has about a million people living here full-time. There are a lot of people who come here in the fall when the crops are harvested, but for the most part this is kind of a sleepy little backwater."

Imri smiled at the fondness in Yacek's voice. "You seem to like it here."

"I do." The older Jedi laughed. "I was never much for the more adventurous parts of Jedi life. I'm a perfectly adequate duelist, but I really like talking to new people. The people on this planet had a terrible tragedy over a century ago, and it's shaped them ever since. They distrust strangers, and all of their children participate in a career-type system where they pick their jobs at a young age and train in a certain specialty. It can make them seem to be a little standoffish, since most people stick to the people in their families or career paths." Yacek shook his head. "Just don't be surprised if they seem a little cold when you talk to them. Also, they tolerate us here in the temple, but the Dalnans don't have a lot of love for the Jedi."

"You know, Master Nyla told us this yesterday. Has something happened to make the people more suspicious recently? We have a friend from Dalna, and he's not like that at all," Vernestra said with a frown. "Honesty Weft. He was on the *Steady Wing* with us and made the trip to Starlight Beacon with us for the dedication. I don't suppose you know him?"

"Weft . . . Ah, the former ambassador's son? Yes, I will say his father was very different than many of the people who live here. He was an advocate for joining the Republic, and I think his death was a large reason they went through with it. Other than that, I'm not sure. The people here have always seemed wary of us, but I suppose it may have gotten worse since the Great Disaster. Everyone everywhere is a bit on edge since the Nihil began wreaking havoc, even if Dalna has been fortunate to never have a direct attack. Anyway, whenever you're ready we can take the landspeeder into town. The vice president has agreed to meet with us and answer any questions we might have. I'm hoping he can give us a better idea of what might have happened to the missing families."

Imri stood and brushed the crumbs off the front of his tabard. As he stood, the tooka climbed onto his shoulder, digging in its claws to remain steady. The pain was bracing, and Imri gritted his teeth. "I'm ready. Um, what about Gemmy here?"

Yacek shrugged. "It seems like he wants to ride along, so if you don't mind you should just go with it. Tookas are great at keeping the pests out of the temple, but once they've made up their minds, there's really nothing to do about it."

Imri scratched Gemmy's head, and the feline responded by making a strange growly sound low in his throat. "I don't mind." The truth was, he was glad for the tooka. He'd woken feeling a little sad and out of sorts, and Gemmy was going a long way toward setting that to rights.

They made their way to the landspeeder, a newer model that started with a purr. Vernestra and Yacek sat up front and chatted while Imri watched the landscape go by. Rows and rows of bushes lined each side of the road, workers walking through the rows and hoeing, watering, and trimming the blue-leafed gnostra berry bushes that were Dalna's lifeblood. Imri had learned long before—right before their ill-fated trip on the *Steady Wing*, to be exact—that the entire economy of Dalna revolved around the fruit. A bad season could send the entire planet into a spiral, and it was one of the reasons they had decided to join the Republic, after all. The central government was good at making sure every member planet had what it needed.

It wasn't long before they left the rolling berry fields behind and came out onto a vast plain. Far-off mountains were visible, the peaks snowcapped even though it was the warm season on Dalna. Imri thought he saw steam coming from one of the mountains, and when he mentioned it, Yacek glanced at him over his shoulder.

"Yeah, that's the volcano. Dalna is a relatively young planet, and it has a very active volcanic system. There are a few scientists here on the planet studying it, but there's nothing to worry about. There hasn't been a real eruption in nearly three hundred years."

The rest of the trip passed quickly, and before Imri knew it, they were pulling up to the city itself, which was much smaller than Imri had imagined.

Yacek had tried to prepare them for Saludad, but it was less a city and more a large town. Neat little houses in an array of purples and pinks pushed up against each other, and the streets were still mostly dirt. Yacek stopped the landspeeder in front of a house that was only slightly bigger than the ones on either side, and blue instead of lavender like its neighbors, the balconies on the front of the house boasting an array of fruiting plants. Imri recognized only a handful of them, and as he climbed out of the landspeeder, Gemmy leapt off his shoulder to chase a furry puffball creature that took off down the narrow alley between houses.

"Don't worry. He'll be back," Yacek said with a smile.

"Should I wait outside for him?" Imri asked.

"You can if you want," Vernestra said. "I don't expect we'll be very long."

Imri nodded, sitting down on the steps while Vernestra and Yacek entered the building. There was no sign designating it as anything special, and Imri found that odd. Didn't government buildings usually have signs?

Even though he'd just woken up, Imri found himself dozing a little in the warm sun. He was wondering if he should go looking for Gemmy when he felt something that caused him to open his eyes and hold up his hand.

Imri's hand closed around a small rock that someone had thrown at him. When he turned to look at the culprit, he dropped the stone and his face broke out in a big smile.

"Honesty! How have you been?" Imri said, climbing to his feet. Honesty Weft hadn't changed that much since Imri had seen him last. He'd grown a little taller and filled out a bit, but he still had that wide-eyed, scared look about him, even if he carried himself much more confidently than before.

Honesty smiled, wide and welcoming. "I thought that was you. Sorry, I couldn't resist. I am glad you caught it, but I'm even happier it really is you." The two boys met in the middle of the dusty street, Honesty greeting Imri by clapping him on the shoulder in the manner of the frontier. "It would've been awkward explaining to some random Padawan why I was throwing rocks at him."

"Yeah, not the best way to make friends," Imri said with a smile.

"What are you doing here in front of the vice president's office?" Honesty asked. "Did the Nihil finally take someone important?"

Imri leaned back a little in shock. "The Nihil really are kidnapping people?"

Honesty's mirth drained away, and he looked up and down the street nervously. "It's not proven, just rumors. . . . You're really here about that? Good."

"What's going on? Yacek said that no one on Dalna would want to talk to us, but if the Nihil are a problem, you should say something. You know we can help, right?"

"We . . . Vernestra is here?" Honesty said, looking at the closed door of the vice president's house. Imri couldn't tell if Honesty was blushing or if it was just the effect of the too-warm sunshine. Honesty turned back to Imri. "Okay, maybe we should talk. But not here. You're staying at the Jedi temple, right?" Imri nodded. "Okay, I'll come by right before sunset. I have a friend who knows about all of this more than I do, and I'll have to see if I can convince her to share what she knows."

"You should know," Imri said, a sudden lump in his throat taking him by surprise, "we're here because they took Avon."

"Who? The Nihil?" At Imri's nod Honesty's fearful expression melted into one of horror. "But, how?"

"They attacked Haileap and they took Avon for some reason. We don't think it's because she's the daughter of a senator, but there's definitely something strange going on."

"You really need to hear Sha'nai's story, then. We've tried telling others but there's someone . . . stopping anyone from helping. Someone powerful."

"Do you know who?" Imri asked, a sudden chill catching him by surprise. He felt as though he were being watched, but a glance up and down the street revealed they were all alone. Honesty's fear was contagious.

"No, but let's not discuss this here. I'll be by later. And try not to worry, Imri. If there's anyone who can take care of themselves, it's Avon."

Imri watched Honesty walk away and tried to convince himself that the boy was right.

CHAPTER ELEVEN

Vernestra didn't get frustrated very often. Not even Imri, who was sometimes a bit slow to grasp concepts that she found relatively simple, could push Vernestra out of the tranquil sense of self she worked hard to cultivate.

The Dalnan vice president, a man named Hackrack Bep, had taken Vernestra right to aggravated in less than a handful of minutes.

She and Yacek had met with the vice president, a Theelin with spotted bronze skin and dark green hair. He smiled politely at Vernestra as she talked, as though she were reciting a lunch menu, not detailing the aftermath of a Nihil attack.

"Very intriguing, Jedi, but I fail to see how this concerns Dalna? We have no dealings with Haileap, other than the occasional hauler that might stop over there while transporting our cargos to market."

"Dalna seems to have some missing residents just like Haileap. We thought you might have some information about where the families had gone."

"Well, there are no missing families on Dalna. I think I would know if there were. And there are also no Nihil. In fact, there haven't been any issues with the Nihil for months," Hackrack said with a wide grin. Vernestra could sense that he was hiding something, and it was big. But no matter how many questions she asked or how much she brought up the facts, the man refused to acknowledge anything even close to families going missing, and definitely nothing concerning the Nihil.

Finally Yacek, sensing that this was a dead end, stood with a polite smile. "Thank you, Vice President Bep. If we have any further questions we'll return."

"Of course, of course," the other man said. "But you

won't find any issues here. Dalna is safe and sound. No need to bring any more Jedi here."

Vernestra took a deep breath and let it out as she followed Yacek out of the building. "Well, what now?"

"Did you learn anything?" Imri asked. The tooka was once more lying across his shoulders, the big cat purring as he burrowed into the top of Imri's tabard.

"Just that the vice president has an uneasy relationship with the truth," Vernestra said, unable to keep the frustration from her voice.

"It's a good thing I have a lead, then," Imri said. He quickly filled Vernestra in on his reunion with Honesty, and some of her annoyance melted away.

"Well, thank the Force," Vernestra said. "Maybe he can help us. I don't get it. Why would the vice president lie to us like that?"

"Don't forget that the Dalnans fear the Jedi," Yacek said. "I mentioned there was a long-ago incident, and the Dalnans still blame the Jedi for things going badly."

"Really?" Imri said with a frown. "Did you look it up in the archives?"

"Yep," Yacek said, crossing his arms. "Well, at least we tried. Lyssa could only find snippets of reports and a single journal entry from one of the Jedi who came here to build the temple. The rest is secured and requires a special clearance from the Council."

"So whatever happened here must have been pretty serious," Vernestra murmured.

Yacek nodded. "Lyssa said she'd never seen an entry catalogued like the one on Dalna. We put in a request to view the full file, but that was months ago, and we still haven't heard anything back."

"Well, I suppose we should go back to the temple and wait for Honesty to come by with his friend. Hopefully they can shed some light on what's happening here."

"More waiting," Imri said with a groan, the tooka yowling in sympathy. Yacek patted the Padawan's shoulder.

"Sometimes the only thing a Jedi can do is wait for the Force to reveal the next steps. Tell you what, I'll make you spicy noodles for lunch, and then we can duel a bit. At least it won't be wasted time."

They climbed into the landspeeder, heading back to

the temple. Vernestra took deep breaths to try to push her irritation to the side. Yacek was right. The Force would lead them to Avon. Vernestra had to believe that.

She just hoped they would find the girl sooner rather than later.

Avon didn't want to have fun helping Royce fix the *Poisoned Barb*, which was the name of the ship they were currently on. But the truth was, she loved fixing things, almost as much as she loved inventing. And there was a lot on the ship that Royce had to fix.

Avon had met a Siniteen or two in her life, but she'd never met one who wasn't a doctor or professor of some sort. When Avon asked Royce why he'd joined the Nihil, he laughed.

"Because they were hiring, of course." It seemed to be a joke that Avon didn't get, and at her confusion the man had rubbed his hand over his large cranium. "The truth is, I'm afraid I'm a bit like you. I'm an inventor and a tinkerer, and the Path engines are . . . well, they're fascinating. The way they process calculations shouldn't work, and yet it does. Of course, without new Paths to feed the naviport, we're limited in what we can safely do, but life is short, and better to die in glory than to waste away forgotten."

Whenever Avon pressed for more information, Royce would just tell her to recalibrate the navigation matrix or reset the timing on the sublight engines, so Avon found all her questions answered with extra work. But when she worked alongside Royce, he was naturally more forthcoming, keeping up a running dialogue in the wake of her silence. That was how she learned that the ship comprised all that was left of Kara Xoo's Tempest. The Quarren in the throne room was the Tempest Runner, and what had originally been over a hundred ships had been whittled down to this single vessel, the *Poisoned Barb*, Kara's ship.

The Jedi and the Republic had broken the Nihil, and now they were running for their lives.

The work wasn't all beneficial, though. Avon tried a few times to get away to use one of the comm units to call for help, but each time Royce found her very quickly and threatened to mash her fingers with a hydrospanner or promised some other bit of violence. He never acted on it, but after the third time, Avon decided it was better for her to be a little choosier about trying to sneak off. She didn't want to test the grouchy engineer too much.

Avon was in the middle of redoing the wiring on the atmospheric mixer, which was stuck at a much lower level of humidity than Kara and the members of other amphibious species liked, when an alarm went off. Avon looked over to Royce, who seemed unbothered by the sudden noise.

"What's that about?" Avon asked.

"It looks like we're back at home base. Kara doesn't like to hit too many spots before laying low for a while. It's dangerous to be a Nihil these days. Well, more dangerous than usual."

"Let's go, pup," said Deva, walking down the hallway toward where Avon and Royce were working. "You need to get back with your friends for the moment."

Avon didn't argue. Working with Royce had reminded her of the benefit of listening, so she followed Deva back to the part of the cargo hold where they kept the other kids.

When Avon entered and the door shut behind her, they all surrounded her, their eyes wide.

"We thought you were dead," Petri said.

"Did they torture you?" Krylind asked, her gaze traveling up and down Avon, looking for injuries.

"No, I just helped their main engineer repair some stuff on the ship. It's amazing this thing even flies, to be honest," Avon said. "But I did learn something about the ship that could be useful."

She quickly filled the other kids in on what she had learned. Avon was in the middle of explaining the Nihil structure of command when the door opened once more. A pale-skinned human Avon didn't recognize pointed a blaster at them as he entered the room.

"All right, kiddos, here's how this is going to go. You're going to follow Yeet there off of the ship. Raise your hand, Yeet."

A silver-skinned Meerian with ropey gold locks of hair raised her hand and lumbered toward a door at the back of the cargo hold, now wide open, and off the ship. The kids lined up behind her and followed without a word. Avon's heart pounded as she walked, her palms sweat-slicked. For the past day she had focused on the tasks at hand, not thinking about the future, but walking down the boarding ramp, Avon could only spin out possible outcomes.

None of them were very good.

They disembarked into an open field, the waist-high grasses golden. There was a slight breeze, and the air smelled sweet and clean. The sky was a pale blue, and puffy clouds broke up the blue space. Two moons hung in the sky, a round one that looked very near and a smaller one that was only half full. Avon suddenly wished J-6 was with her. She would have known what planet they were on from analyzing the landscape and sky. Avon could only posit that they hadn't traveled very far from Haileap. They hadn't jumped into hyperspace, and she wondered if it was because they were afraid to use the Path engines, which were risky without the preloaded calculations. The Nihil had avoided capture by the Republic for a very long time because their Path engines didn't use the calculations provided by navigational beacons or even navicomputers but rather time-phased calculations provided by the woman they'd called the Oracle. Avon had tried asking Royce about the woman, who the holos reported was able to calculate numerous hyperspace jumps for any moment in time, but he'd just grunted and changed the subject.

Avon couldn't help wondering where they were. Were they even in Republic-controlled space anymore?

A sudden wave of hopelessness washed over her, and she had to blink quickly to chase away the hot tears that stung her eyes. She wouldn't show these Nihil any weakness. She knew that would be the opposite of helpful.

Avon and the rest of the kids were herded into a group with several others, some of them much younger than Avon. A few of the littler ones were crying. The kids all wore vastly different clothing, some dressed in the attire of the frontier and others, like Avon, wearing fashions more common to the Inner Rim. There were about twenty kids altogether, and there were three other ships already docked in the field, each of them smaller than the *Poisoned Barb*.

Were the ships all part of Kara Xoo's Tempest? Royce had told Avon that Kara was down to a single ship, but Avon wasn't one to take anything a Nihil told her at face value. So where had these other ships come from? Was this all that remained of the Nihil?

Avon tried to listen, to pay attention to what was

happening around her. But it was hard. Some of the Nihil were speaking in Galactic Basic, but Avon also caught snatches of what sounded like Huttese and half a dozen other languages she didn't recognize at all. If only she had J-6, she thought once more. The droid would've been able to translate it all for her.

Yeet stepped up to the edge of a dais and stopped. They'd herded all the children into a large group, blasters all around. On the dais Kara Xoo stood, hands on her hips. Her face tentacles danced as everyone gathered, and her mottled, rust-colored skin glimmered wetly in the sunshine.

"Excellent, excellent! Welcome, recruits. It is so good to have you."

The woman's words sent a ripple of confusion through the group of children. Some of them asked their friends what she'd said, and there was a moment as everyone reacted. Avon was the only one not confused. This was just as she'd thought, and the confirmation of Avon's suspicions raised its own challenges. She hadn't wanted to join the Nihil, and she still didn't. So how was she going to get out of this?

"Of course, you are not recruits quite yet," Kara Xoo continued with a harsh laugh. "That will come later. You see all of the Nihil surrounding you? Remember the faces of your minders. Because they will pay the price for your failure. Your job is to prove to us that you can be great Nihil."

"What if we don't want to be Nihil?" called an older Mirialan girl, tiny dots tattooed in a complicated pattern across her cheeks. The girl's hair hung down her back, and even though she looked nothing like Vernestra, Avon suddenly wished the Jedi were there. Vernestra and Imri could handle the Nihil easily. They wouldn't know what hit them.

"If you *aren't* Nihil, you are cattle," she said, pointing across the field to a grouping of ramshackle huts. People moved in between the buildings, their shoulders slumped. There were fields nearby, and the meaning was clear. There was no escape from the Nihil, but maybe they could choose their future.

"All right, let's go," said the human Nihil from before, his blaster poking Avon in the small of her back.

"Not that one, Squib," someone called. A human woman

approached, the Shani Deva following along behind her, both of them intent on Avon. "Deva tells me that you finally found me a proper assistant."

"I got different orders," Squib said. He spat on the ground, and Avon danced away to keep it from hitting her. "My Strike needs members, and I already called this group of recruits."

"Not likely," Deva said, showing her teeth to the man. "But I'm happy to take this one to the arena."

The man's attitude changed immediately. "No, no, that's not necessary. Take the girl. I still have the other three. They look like they can be toughened up."

Yeet and Squib walked off, Krylind, Petri, and Liam walking ahead of them. Avon watched them go, a little sad that she hadn't been able to fulfill her promise to save them, even if they didn't seem to like her much, but a chilly hand on Avon's shoulder pulled her attention back to the women standing over her.

"Avon Sunvale, this is Dr. Zadina Mkampa. She's working on a very special project, and you have the chance to help her," Deva said.

Avon swallowed dryly as she studied the woman. Her

skin was a lighter brown than Avon's, and she wore her dark hair braided down her back. There were strange circuits along her jawline that seemed to grow up from her chest, and Avon wondered what kind of terrible accident the woman had been in that her body would need so many cybernetic augmentations. The hand the woman held out looked more like a cyborg's than a human's.

"A delight, Ms. Sunvale, to be certain. But before I take you as my lab assistant, I must ask you: what do you know about the properties of ambivalent crystal resonations and their associated uses?"

Avon's heart pounded. She glanced over to where Krylind, Petri, and Liam were being led to a big block building with the rest of the kidnapped kids. They weren't recruits. The Nihil had snatched them from their homes the same way they'd taken Avon and the other kids. It would be easy to lie to this doctor, pretend she had no idea what the woman was talking about.

But Avon had never been any good at playing stupid, and she didn't want to start now.

"I've been studying the work of Annabet Ursul for the past year. Although I find the theory of resonate friction to be hard to prove in the lab when taking into account the varying matrix structures of most crystalline substances. Sure, quartz correlates, but rarer structures like those belonging to kyber and lystrater never harmonize in quite the same way."

There was a moment where Avon was afraid she'd said too much. She slipped her hand into her pocket, the comforting weight of Imri's kyber crystal giving her a measure of strength and calm.

"Deva," Dr. Mkampa said, her eyes shining, "she is absolutely perfect. Ms. Sunvale, would you like to be my assistant?"

"What happens if I say no?" Avon asked, her voice low.

"Oh, well, I suppose you can return to the oversight of Yeet and Squib. But I will warn you. They keep . . . losing recruits. Tragically."

Avon swallowed past the lump of fear in her throat and gave a tremulous smile.

"I'd love to be your assistant," she said.

"Brilliant," Dr. Mkampa said. "Let's get you something more appropriate to wear, and we'll get to work."

By the time the sun set, Vernestra had meditated three times, gone through the entirety of the reports on the Nihil from the past few days with Lyssa, and sparred with Imri and Yacek both. Vernestra had invited Master Nyla to their contest, as well, but the older Jedi begged off after she saw Vernestra duel.

"I see why you made Knight so young, Jedi," the older Twi'lek said with a laugh. "Watching you work is breathtaking, and I'd not like you reminding me of my age. No, I am content to watch you younger lot train with each other. But I am happy to offer insight, if you'd like?"

And so Vernestra spent the rest of the afternoon dueling Yacek, Master Nyla critiquing their form and explaining to Imri some of the rarer techniques being used. The third time Vernestra bested Yacek, he held up his hands in surrender. "Solah! I know when I'm outmatched. Lyssa was smart to bury herself in her research and avoid the embarrassment."

Vernestra accepted his surrender with good humor before going to try out the steam baths, apparently the pride of the temple. After a good long soak, Vernestra felt a bit better. Still on edge, but less frustrated.

As the sun sank toward the horizon, the temperature dropping when it disappeared, Vernestra went to the ship to check on J-6. She hadn't seen the droid all day, and it seemed odd. It didn't usually take that long for a droid to charge.

When Vernestra boarded the *Wishful Thinking*, she found the droid in the pilot's seat, scanning public bands.

"Jay-Six, have you been here the whole time?" Vernestra asked. She'd somewhat forgotten about the droid. Her attention had been all for finding out about the possible location of the missing Dalnan families so they could find Avon.

"Yes, I have. I see that you did not bring me the oil I requested. Either way, did you know there are approximately two million distinct comm channels throughout this region of the galaxy? Most have a range of three or four sectors, perhaps a bit further now that Starlight Beacon is there to boost signals." The droid turned to Vernestra. "I have been running an algorithm to see which channels Avon is most likely to use to send a call for help, and I have narrowed it down to three thousand five hundred and sixty-three frequencies. Of that number about half have a record of at least once being used by the Nihil. So I have been scanning all of them for the past day."

"And?" Vernestra said, a twinge of hope entering the word.

Droids did not sigh. They didn't breathe; so there was no exhalation of annoyance or despair that would allow them to make such a noise. And yet, the sound J-6 made sounded an awful lot like a sigh.

"I've found nothing. Not just a lack of Avon, but a lack of Nihil chatter altogether. Whatever they are up to, they are being very quiet about it."

"Well, keep on it. It's more than we've been able to do,

so far," Vernestra said, the news more disappointing than it should have been. Vernestra wanted to find Avon, but the rational part of her mind knew how unlikely that was. It was a big galaxy. How could they find a single girl when she could be almost anywhere?

The sound of a pair of speeder bikes approaching pulled Vernestra from her worry, and she walked to the boarding ramp of the ship. As she disembarked, Imri exited the front of the temple, a savory pastry pocket in his hand.

"Once we find Avon we should petition for some time at one of the temple outposts," Imri said, holding out the pastry pocket for Vernestra to try. At her refusal he shrugged and took another bite. "The food here is even better than Starlight's. Yacek may not be a great duelist, but he's an amazing cook. He said that the food in the temple on Hon-Tallos is even better. I think I'd like to visit there."

"That's a good idea. Look, there's Honesty," Vernestra said, unable to keep the smile off her face as the boy climbed off of the speeder bike and removed his helmet. Even though it had been a while since they'd been stranded on Wevo, Vernestra felt like it had been just yesterday that she'd been waving goodbye as Honesty departed Starlight for Coruscant so he could testify on behalf of the Dalnan delegation. All the other members had died in the disaster aboard the *Steady Wing*, and it had been Honesty's impassioned plea that had led to both of the Nihil responsible being sent to spend the rest of their lives on a prison hauler.

As Honesty approached, Vernestra took a moment to study his companion. A Pantoran girl, her blue skin radiant in the fading sunlight, pushed a lock of hair behind her ear. She looked vaguely familiar, and Vernestra wondered if she'd had family on the *Steady Wing*. There had been a Pantoran woman as part of the Dalnan delegation, but Vernestra found that she couldn't remember the woman's name.

"Imri! Hey, Vernestra," Honesty said with a wide grin. He looked relaxed, something Vernestra couldn't ever remember seeing before. He'd been a nervous sort of person, and Vernestra marveled once more how much could change in such a short time.

"Honesty! Well met. Look how tall you've gotten," Vernestra said, thumping her chest with a smile. Honesty grinned and returned the greeting.

"I've been busy. Vernestra, Imri, I want you to meet Sha'nai Plouth. She's, uh, my partner."

Imri looked from Sha'nai to Honesty and back. "Um, you're engaged?"

The Pantoran girl laughed. "Don't look so horrified. It's not that kind of partnership. Part of our apprenticeship is being paired with someone who complements you. Both Honesty and I are trainees with the protection corps."

"Oh, I see," Imri said. "That's kind of neat, to have another apprentice to hang around with."

"Yes, but that's not why we're here," Honesty said, his mirth fading. "We should go inside. This far from the city you're likely to get feral snipes prowling the landscape, not to mention the ice gators, and neither of us are allowed to carry a blaster yet."

"Oh, then let's get inside," Vernestra said.

They entered the temple outpost to find a feast laid out in the common area, Master Nyla and Yacek standing near the spread. As they entered, Master Nyla held out her hands.

"Welcome, Dalnans!" she said, her voice perhaps a bit

too bright. "We prepared an evening repast, and we hope you'll join us."

Honesty and Sha'nai exchanged looks before they nodded. "Thank you," Honesty said. "Your generosity is most appreciated."

"You say that like you're surprised," Imri said, voice low, as they all took seats at the table. "Have you not been here to visit the temple?"

"Once," Honesty said with a sheepish grin. "It was, ah, weird. Dalnans have a long memory, and many still blame the Jedi for the Night of Sorrow."

"Oh? What was that?" Vernestra asked, putting a spoonful of purple steam beans on her plate, the smell making her mouth water. Yacek really was a fabulous cook. Almost as good as Jedi Porter Engle. Vernestra wasn't the fanciful sort, but she imagined a cook-off between the two would leave everyone involved full and happy.

"We aren't supposed to talk about it," Sha'nai said, glancing quickly at Honesty. "It's bad to speak of the dead when it's dark out."

"It was a battle that happened long ago. The Republic and the Jedi answered a call for help when Dalna was newly settled, and there was some confusion. When they arrived things went badly, and a lot of people died," Honesty said, his eyes on his plate. "Sha'nai is right. We aren't supposed to bring it up, but my father always believed history should be shared. There are a lot of people who still blame the Jedi for what happened, although I'm not sure why."

"It doesn't matter," Sha'nai said, clearly uncomfortable with the current conversation. "We're here to talk about the Nihil."

"So, you know something?" Vernestra asked, leaning forward.

Sha'nai nodded. "There was an attack just a few days ago. I saw it."

The girl bit her lip, clearly struggling with something. Imri caught Vernestra's eye, and she gave him a short nod. They'd discovered that Imri was extremely talented at creating Force bonds with people in distress, smoothing their emotions so they could work through things. Vernestra had asked Imri not to do it without consulting her. She was worried it was overstepping a bit in some cases, but Sha'nai could benefit from a little soothing, her fear clearly causing her distress.

Imri reached across the table and rested his hand on Sha'nai's. "If you don't want to tell us, you don't have to. But we're looking for our friend, Avon. The Nihil took her and without your help we might never find her."

"I want to tell you, I really do," Sha'nai said with a heavy sigh. A bit of her distress eased, and she began to breathe easier. "It's just that . . . when we told the security chief he took me to speak to the president, who told us that we needed to let the matter rest. It's a matter of utmost secrecy. I don't want to get in trouble."

"Child, if there is something so big that even your mentor cannot take care of it, you should definitely tell us," Master Nyla said with a frown. "The Jedi are here to help. We may have made mistakes in the past, but we are not those same Jedi."

"The Jedi in the old stories weren't bad," Honesty said with a head shake. "I don't want you to think that. It's more that they . . . didn't fully understand the problem before they rushed in. Sha'nai, I told you that these Jedi aren't like the ones we learn about in the old stories. You can trust them."

The Pantoran girl nodded and took a deep breath. "Okay. One of the things I like to do when I have free time is ride my glider near the Maawat Mountains. They're the mountains south of here, about two hundred kilometers. My glider doesn't go very high, maybe a couple hundred meters or so, but it's a great way to take in the mountain range. Anyway, not too long ago I was flying and I saw . . . well, I saw the Nihil!"

"Wait, the Nihil are here on Dalna?" Yacek said, and Sha'nai shook her head.

"No, they were here, but they're gone. I reported it, and the security chief told me he was going to check it out. But when I followed up later, he told me the security corps would handle it. But I don't think they did anything."

"Do you think your security chief found something there?" Vernestra asked.

Honesty nodded. "It makes the most sense. There have been some reports of ships coming and going at all hours of the night, but the Council and all of the other adults have called it nothing but storm lights, or volcanic gases reacting within the atmosphere. I'm worried that maybe they're keeping the truth from the rest of the people here."

"What about the missing families?" Yacek asked. "Has anyone complained about neighbors disappearing?"

Honesty and Sha'nai exchanged looks before Honesty answered. "There was something about a month or so ago. I went with the security chief to talk to some neighbors of one of the families reported missing, but they said they knew nothing. I think they were scared."

The Jedi at the table all fell silent for a long moment before Master Nyla spoke. "Please do not take this the wrong way, honored Dalnans, but do you trust your security chief?" she asked in a low voice.

Honesty shrugged. "Yes, most definitely. But the new president is odd. She got elected earlier this year and everyone seemed surprised because no one really knew her that well."

"My father doesn't like her," Sha'nai said. "But he doesn't really like anyone who wasn't born here."

"Do you think you can show us this spot?" Vernestra asked.

"Yes," Sha'nai said with a decisive nod. Now that her story was out and no one seemed disinclined to believe her, she was much more relaxed. Either that, or Imri's ability was still working its magic. "It's one of the reasons Honesty wanted to meet you all at dusk. The Maawat Mountains should be in daylight now. Since you all have a ship, it should be easy to find the spot."

"We should go right now," Vernestra said, standing, her food completely forgotten. The rest of the group looked at her for a long moment before standing reluctantly.

Yacek smiled. "Let me wrap up these pastry pockets, and we can be on our way."

It didn't take long for Vernestra, Imri, Sha'nai, Honesty, and Yacek to pile into the *Wishful Thinking*. Lyssa joined them at the last minute, rushing in with a datapad, her hair slightly askew. "Someone should record this for the archives," she said.

Master Nyla decided to stay behind, as the temple outpost was supposed to always have at least a single Jedi in residence. It was a good thing, too. The ship was small, so it was a tight fit even without the Jedi Master, and J-6 seemed disinclined to move from her place in the copilot's seat when they boarded.

"I finally have a process going, and I will not abandon

it now," she said. Yacek's gaze met Vernestra's in surprise.

"I didn't know you had a droid," he said.

"Jay-Six is pretty much her own droid, to be honest. She's friends with Avon."

There wasn't much conversation after that. Imri piloted the shuttle, following Sha'nai's directions to their destination. Yacek passed around the basket of vegetable pies and nice bottles of hygge nectar, and they finished their dinner high above Dalna.

The flight didn't take much more than half an hour. Dalna was a small planet, and their quick trip halfway around the globe only reinforced that fact.

They flew over the area Sha'nai indicated once, twice, everyone crowded around the ship's few viewports to try to get a good look outside. But it seemed much like the land around the temple outpost: various streams, grasslands, a few trees here and there.

"Is there a reason why no one lives in these mountains?" Imri asked as they landed the shuttle in a relatively empty field, a few trees the only thing breaking up the landscape.

"This part of the planet is highly sulfurous. See those springs? They're all hot springs, and the water isn't very good for growing much. Plus, it stinks," Honesty said, sticking his tongue out in disgust.

"This has also been the source of much of the volcanic activity on Dalna, according to records," Lyssa said, tapping on the datapad. "The Maawat Mountains are more a connected linkage of volcanoes than actual mountains, and much of what makes Dalna so perfect for farming gnostra berries is the rich soil and the ambient soil temperature, which averages three to four degrees higher than many places thanks to the incredibly thin planetary crust."

They disembarked from the *Wishful Thinking*, and Vernestra squinted as her eyes adjusted to the sunlight. It was odd going from nighttime to bright early morning. Sublight engines were very fast, but even so, Vernestra had never been on such a small planet. It seemed strange that the Nihil could find something worthwhile on Dalna. There didn't seem to be anything on the planet but berry bushes and farmers who distrusted offworlders.

Sha'nai led the way, pointing out where she'd seen the ships. It was clear someone had been there recently. The grass bore the telltale markings of a large ship touching down, but whether it had been Nihil or someone else wasn't clear.

"What do you think they were doing here, in this field?" Vernestra asked.

"No ideas," Yacek said with a frown. "I'm still trying to figure out why the vice president would lie to us like that. They clearly know that there is some kind of Nihil activity here on Dalna."

"But just what are they doing here?" Lyssa murmured, tapping on her datapad. "I still don't understand why Dalna, of all the locations in this part of the galaxy."

Yacek nodded. "Same. I love this little planet, but I cannot imagine any strategic purpose for being here. Let's split up and see if we can find anything useful."

"Maybe we should ask Jay-Six," Imri said. "She, uh, has a full databank, right?"

"Oh, good idea." Vernestra entered the ship once more to find the droid right where they'd left her. "Jay-Six, do you have any data on Dalna?"

"Some. Avon asked for me to do a skim of the big important things after our adventure on Wevo," the droid said without turning to look back at Vernestra.

"Do you have anything in your databank about the Night of Sorrow?" Vernestra asked. J-6 was quiet for a moment before she responded.

"Nothing about that, sorry. Any other queries?" the droid asked. Her attention was mostly focused on the comm channels streaming past.

"How about the Maawat Mountains?" Vernestra asked.

J-6 hummed. Vernestra wasn't sure droids were supposed to do that, but after a moment the sound stopped. "Yes, I did find something. A geological survey conducted by a Republic survey team over two centuries ago, titled 'Seismic Events and Their Role in Force Confluences.'"

Vernestra frowned. Why would the Republic have anything to do with Force theory, or confluences in the Force? That seemed more like Jedi business. But also, this was similar to what Lyssa had already told them, so it seemed as though J-6 did not have any information beyond what was already easily accessible.

Before Vernestra could ask J-6 to elaborate, there was a shout outside the shuttle. She hurried out, lightsaber drawn, to see Lyssa, Yacek, Imri, Honesty, and Sha'nai all rushing toward the ship. Behind them was a herd of some kind of wild animal. Hundreds of them ran across the clearing, a cloud of dust rising up on all sides. They looked a bit like banthas, only skinnier and with a short blue coat, and the herd was bearing down on the ship.

"Get inside!" Yacek yelled. Vernestra rushed toward him, passing Lyssa as the archivist dashed into the ship. Vernestra would have done the same, but if that herd rammed into the *Wishful Thinking,* the ship would be severely damaged. She had to redirect the animals.

Vernestra holstered her lightsaber and planted her boots in the dirt. And waited. Honesty sprinted past, followed by Sha'nai and Yacek, and Imri came in last, huffing and puffing. He didn't halt or even slow his stride, just gave Vernestra a nod of understanding as he climbed aboard the ship.

Vernestra heard the whine of the engines starting, satisfaction surging through her. Smart Padawan. The sooner he could get the ship in the air, the better the chance that the approaching beasts wouldn't get to damage it.

But Vernestra had other issues. She had to move a frightened herd of beasts, and it was going to take all her ability to do it.

Vernestra reached for the Force, pulling it into and around her. Her goal was to redirect the herd, but she also had to be able to protect her body. The hooves and horns of the animals would make short work of soft Mirialan flesh, and Vernestra did not want to chance getting injured. She still had to find Avon, and she couldn't do that if she was hurt. Or worse, dead.

Once Vernestra was ready, she used the Force to reach for the lead animals of the herd. She gently pushed them to the right, urging them around her and the *Wishful Thinking*. It was harder than it looked. Vernestra wasn't building a wall; the Force didn't do such things. It was all motion and potential, and the way Vernestra influenced that was by gently pushing each of the beasts to the right one at a time. It was a bit like navigating a crowd, only Vernestra was pushing them around her. It was difficult work, and very quickly she realized that the herd was bigger than she'd thought. She was going to get tired from using the Force to nudge the animals to the side long before the massive herd had passed.

"Vern!" came the shout behind her. Vernestra hazarded a quick look over her shoulder to see Yacek waving at her from the open boarding ramp. Imri had managed to power up the ship and lift off. The edge of the boarding ramp was maybe two meters off the ground. A difficult jump for most, but no problem for a Jedi.

Vernestra didn't hesitate. She turned and leapt for the boarding ramp, pushing off of the ground with the Force so she landed easily next to Yacek.

"Nicely done," the other Knight said with a grin. "The boolsa are harmless, but when they're panicked like this there's no stopping them."

"Do you know what startled them?" Vernestra asked, and Yacek shook his head.

"We saw them running toward us, and we hightailed it back to the ship."

"Imri," Vernestra called through the ship. "Can you take us in the direction the herd came from?"

"No problem, Vern!" Imri called from the pilot's seat. He swung the craft around, flying over the startled beasts. They didn't have to go far to find the cause of the animals' disturbance.

A short way from where they'd landed, where Sha'nai had reported seeing the Nihil, was a ramshackle building.

It didn't look like much, but it was definitely out of place. A couple of bright blue lizards the size of landspeeders were attacking the building, their sharp teeth and claw-like hands tearing away the flimsy metal that made up the exterior.

"Um, ice gators, I presume?" Vernestra asked.

Next to her, Yacek nodded. "Yeah. They should have already gone to ground for the day, but it looks like there's something in there that they want."

"You said that no one lived out here in these mountains, right?" Vernestra said.

Yacek nodded once more. "Are you thinking what I am?"

"That it's a good day to fight an ice gator?" Vernestra asked.

"That is definitely not what I was thinking," Yacek said, eyes wide. "But someone must be inside of there. And yes, we should probably stop those reptiles from hurting whoever it is."

Lyssa poked her head around the corner. "There's only two of them. I'm sure you'll do fine. And at this time of day they should be slow and sleepy."

"*We'll* do fine," Yacek said in a low voice, and Lyssa gave him a nervous smile.

" 'We'?"

"We," Yacek said, stressing the single word.

Lyssa swallowed, her nervousness clear. "What if I left my lightsaber behind?"

Yacek pulled a lightsaber from inside his tabard and flipped it to the archivist, who caught it with a sigh. Yacek shrugged. "I thought you might have overlooked it, so I made sure to grab it for you."

"You know I hate fighting," Lyssa said. She wasn't pouting, but it was a near thing.

"This will be good practice," Yacek answered with a smile.

Vernestra pressed her lips together to stifle her laughter, then yelled for Imri to find them a place to land.

"Let's ice these gators."

FOURTEEN

Avon followed the woman, Dr. Mkampa, to a low building some ways away from the main compound. Part of her wondered what the Nihil would do to the rest of her group. It didn't seem like they wanted to hurt any of them. If they had they could've easily gotten rid of them on board the *Poisoned Barb*. But it seemed strange to think they'd been recruited somehow. Why would the Nihil have to recruit kids? They were the scariest thing on the frontier. They took whatever they wanted, and even the Republic had reason to fear them. They were powerful in a way not too many were. It seemed like people, at least a certain sort, should be lining up to join them.

Avon's attention was pulled away from her musings and to the door opening before her. Dr. Mkampa gestured for her to enter.

"I don't think I have to tell you that any attempt at escape will be met with a swift and painful punishment," the woman said. "It's primitive, but the Nihil are somewhat known for their simplicity. It's one of the things I appreciate about them."

Avon said nothing, just took in the room around her. It was a lab of sorts. There was a crystal matrix analyzer and a number of oscilloscopes, as well as a Mertigan, which was used to measure compounded energy output from crystals. None of the machines looked new, and a few showed signs of having been repaired. It should have been exciting, to find a scientist who needed Avon's help after the harrowing experience of being kidnapped, but all Avon could think about was the people who had once owned this equipment.

What had happened to them? Were they still alive?

Maybe it was better not to think about such things.

Dr. Mkampa pointed to a pile of dust sitting in a jar.

"You and I have a very, very big job before us. I need to ascertain the correct frequency to create a chain reaction of vibrations in that ferrous crystal aggregate."

"Wouldn't that just be the crystals' base unit extrapolated to Layne's coefficient?" Avon said, peering at the dust on the plate of the Mertigan.

"Where did they find you again?" Dr. Mkampa said, her dark brows arched and her arms crossed. Avon suddenly wondered if she'd revealed too much, and she coughed delicately.

"I don't suppose I could have a glass of water? I'm afraid I'm pretty thirsty."

"Of course. Follow me, and I'll show you the rest of the lab while we get it."

There wasn't much to the lab beyond what Dr. Mkampa had already shown Avon. There was a crystal splicer and an actual fusion matrix, which was used to create synthetic crystals that could focus and channel power. Such a machine was rare, and Avon had begged Professor Glenna Kip more times than she could remember to go see the fusion matrix kept on Coruscant. Professor Kip had joked about not being welcome on Coruscant, and the matter had been put to bed. But looking at the machine now, Avon wondered once again who had owned it.

"This will be your room," Dr. Mkampa said, gesturing toward a room with a single cot and nothing else. "I suppose you'll need things. A comb, a change of clothing." She seemed unsure, like she didn't really know what kinds of things a kid would need. Avon didn't say anything, and the woman continued. "We share in the spoils of war just like everyone else, although those have been slim pickings, lately. I'll make sure we find something suitable for you, regardless."

"What do you do for the Nihil? I mean, the Path drives aren't powered by a crystal matrix. I know because I looked at one. In fact, nothing they use has such a sophisticated power system . . ." Avon said, her voice trailing off.

"That, I am afraid, is none of your concern." The doctor gave Avon a chilling look, one that made Avon feel like the woman was cataloging every single bit of her, dissecting her with her eyes. Avon said nothing, remembering how holding her tongue had led to Royce telling her more than he would've otherwise, and she was surprised when it worked on Dr. Mkampa, as well.

"But I will say that I used to be a munitions expert before I came to work for the Nihil. Are you familiar with Soika?" At Avon's head shake, the woman sighed. "It was a beautiful war there, the kind of endless civil war that gives a scientist numerous opportunities for experimentation. Anyway, the war did end when the Republic intervened, and I was left homeless and without an occupation. I suppose I could have gone to one of the stuffy universities, but I've always had more of an interest in the . . . practical applications of my field. Hmm, looks like we don't have any water, but here's a bottle of sweetdrink. Bubbles or no bubbles?"

The scientist was bent with her head in a chiller, and it was such a normal sight that Avon suddenly felt like crying. This might not be her first time being kidnapped—she'd gone through a much more harrowing experience last time—but she was so out of her depth that she felt a deep sense of despair.

"Bubbles, if you have it," Avon said, hoping her voice didn't sound as shaky as she felt.

Dr. Mkampa opened the bottle with her hand, something Avon couldn't have done in a hundred years, not even with Jedi abilities. The woman had no need of a bottle opener, most likely due to her augmentations. It was a good lesson. Dr. Mkampa was stronger than she looked.

"How did you, um, end up with so many cybernetic bits?" Avon said, accepting the bottle and taking an experimental drink. It was good, a sort of fruity flavor she didn't recognize, and the sugar hitting her belly reminded her that she hadn't eaten in a while.

"Ahh, a terrible accident, to be sure. Sometimes when one is pursuing a line of logic, things can become rather fraught, but that is the moment when it is most important to follow through," the woman said with a smile. She was very pretty, but there was something off-putting about her. It was her eyes. They were strangely vacant, and looking into them for too long gave Avon a peculiar feeling that she didn't like.

"Enough of this," Dr. Mkampa said, clapping her hands as though to wake herself up. "We have work to do. I suppose you are going to tell me you are also hungry? As for that, food will be brought to us so that we don't have to fight for our rations. But that means we have to earn our keep. Are you familiar with how to chamber powders and liquids into a Heddle construct?"

Avon nodded and let Dr. Mkampa lead her to yet another table set in an alcove in the back. The woman explained the order of how to put the materials together, but Avon was only half listening, because the more she looked at the pieces of the device, the more she realized she was looking at the Nihil's gas bombs, these just waiting to be assembled.

Any hopes Avon might have had about not causing harm evaporated right then and there. This doctor, who seemed smart and competent, was helping the Nihil kill people.

And if Avon followed her instructions, she would be doing exactly the same thing.

CHAPTER FIFTEEN

The Jedi did not waste time before going after the ice gators. Imri kept the shuttle in a low hover a short distance away from where the reptiles were tearing at the ramshackle cabin while the other Jedi jumped out of the *Wishful Thinking*. They ran straight toward the beasts, engaging them quickly.

Vernestra powered up her lightsaber as she ran, the purple blade singing, while Yacek and Lyssa did the same. Yacek's lightsaber was a strong, brilliant green, while Lyssa's was a blue so pale it was almost white. The sound of the plasma blades powering up was enough to draw the

attention of the two ice gators, which swung their massive heads toward the Jedi.

"*Aiiieee!*" Lyssa yelled, swinging her lightsaber as one snapped its jaws at her. The tip of the blade caught the animal's snout, slicing cleanly through leathery blue skin and razor-sharp teeth. The beast howled in pain and lumbered backward, away from the Jedi's lightsaber.

"Let's try to drive them away without killing them if we can," Yacek said as the ice gator before Lyssa turned and ran off toward the trees. Vernestra twisted the bezel on her lightsaber, the purple blade melting into a whip. The ice gator still tearing at the lopsided building before her turned around, and keeping her distance, Vernestra swung her weapon, the end of it sizzling where it made contact with the ground less than a meter from the ice gator. She wanted to chase the creature off, not injure it.

The ice gator roared in response, and Vernestra was afraid she was going to have to fight the animal, but then it let out a smaller, croaking sound and turned and lumbered away, retreating back into the tree line rather than continuing the fight.

"It's past your bedtime anyway!" Yacek called, powering

down his lightsaber and holstering it. Lyssa and Vernestra did the same, and relief washed over Vernestra. The ice gators were impressive creatures, and she was glad she didn't have to kill either of them.

"I think I'm going to go back to pulling up any information we have on the Maawat Mountains," Lyssa said, looking a bit ill from the experience. She returned to the ship while Yacek and Vernestra approached the ramshackle cabin, which looked even worse now that the sides bore additional damage from the ice gators' claws.

"Really glad we didn't have to fight them," Yacek said, looking at the slices in the metal.

The Jedi did not approach the ramshackle structure with any kind of caution. Vernestra knew it was a terrible risk to take. But when she pushed the door open, they found a perfectly empty space.

"Guess nobody's home," Yacek said.

Vernestra frowned, because there was something about the space that felt off to her. It wasn't the rumpled blanket on the cot or the remains of a fire in the middle of the room, right below a smoke hole in the ceiling. It was the dried bundle of flowers tied up and placed in a metal container that looked like a broken piece of a ship.

"Do you recognize those flowers?" Vernestra asked Yacek, pointing to the metal cup they sat in.

"Hmm, they look like lompop. It's a wildflower that grows in some of the meadows around here."

"Are they seasonal?"

"I think so. Summer flowers. We had them down at our elevation a few weeks ago. Someplace like up here, they should be in bloom right now."

There was a thumping noise, and Vernestra and Yacek both pulled their lightsabers, not powering them up, just holding them while they waited to hear the noise again. It didn't take long. There was another thump, and this time it was clear that it came from a cleverly disguised hatch carved into the floor.

Vernestra signaled to Yacek that she was going to open the hatch, and he nodded. Even though she'd already taxed herself greatly not moments before, she easily reached with the Force to pull the hatch up and away.

It flew across the room, and a boy exploded out of the

hidey-hole, his eyes wide with fear. He was a Theelin, his skin a shining bronze mottled with spots and his hair a dark green, the exact same shade as the vice president's.

"Please," the boy said. "Don't kill me."

Avon couldn't sleep. That was no surprise. Instead, she tossed and turned in her small bed, her brain supplying helpful images as to how the canisters could be used. She'd seen the Nihil and their fog of war in action before. Some of their gas canisters knocked people out and confused them. And some were toxic, killing anyone who came into contact with the gas.

Avon thought of the cold way Dr. Mkampa looked at her, and had no doubt the woman could easily create something meant to kill someone. The Soikan civil war had been deadly and brutal, and if that woman had been involved, then that could mean nothing good.

Avon had spent the rest of the evening watching as the woman explained to her how to assemble the bombs on the workbench. It was easy work. Avon could have done it in her sleep. But she didn't want to be responsible for creating something so destructive. Avon loved technology because of the way it could make people's lives better, but Dr. Mkampa was a reminder that not everyone felt that way about science.

Avon had to get away from Dr. Mkampa and all her terrible work before she accidentally helped the woman develop something disastrous.

She waited until all the sounds in the lab had died down to nothing before climbing out of bed and creeping out of her room. The lab was dark, the glow of one of the crystal matrices that Dr. Mkampa was growing the only light. But Avon had memorized the layout of the lab, so it was no problem to creep past the analyzers and out the main door, which wasn't even locked.

That unlocked door worried Avon more than anything else. It meant that Dr. Mkampa wasn't concerned about the rest of the Nihil disturbing her. She was perhaps even more dangerous than Avon had thought.

There were few options for Avon once she was outside of the lab. The wisest course of action would be to send a call for help, but Avon had no idea where the comms might be.

With the exception of the *Poisoned Barb*.

The hulking wreck sat on the far end of the field, smaller ships all around it, and the boarding ramp was down. The twin moons above cast enough light that Avon could easily make her way to the ship, and the auxiliary power must have still been on, from the glimmer of light that appeared through a few of the viewports on the side. But as far as Avon could tell, there didn't seem to be any Nihil about.

For a moment Avon crouched in the grass, heart pounding and palms slicked with fear. But then she thought of all the destructive things a person like Dr. Mkampa could do with a functioning crystal matrix that could be used to power a weapon, and she used that fear to propel her across the short distance to the boarding ramp and back onto the *Poisoned Barb*.

Avon didn't try to be quiet. As soon as she boarded the ship, the sounds of Nihil having some kind of party echoed through the hall, so she opted for speed over stealth. Her time spent working with Royce had given her a good idea of where to go. She wasted no time getting to the comms room, and once she was inside, she locked the door behind her. For a moment she stood there, heart pounding, elation washing over her as she realized she'd done it!

But a single look at the equipment and her heart fell. It was less a comms room and more a collection of components spliced together. The broadcast terminal was ancient, and when Avon tried the Republic channels, she found they were nothing but static.

She'd risked her life to get to the comms room, and it looked like there was no way to even send a message.

Avon took a deep breath and let it out, trying to tamp down her rising panic. She could do this. All she had to do was get a message out some way. The Jedi would find her. She had to believe that.

So she opened up as many channels as she could find and began to broadcast.

"Hello, my name is Avon, and I've been kidnapped by the Nihil. I went missing from Port Haileap, um, I'm not quite sure how many days ago. There are a lot of other kids here, as well, and the Nihil are forcing us to join with them or they're going to enslave us and make us work for them anyway. Please help. I'm located on an unknown planet with two moons."

Avon tried to clear her throat, but then she found herself crying, the stress and fear of the past few days rising at the worst possible moment. She cleared her throat and tried again.

"I'm going to put this message on loop in the hopes that someone can triangulate my location. Please help."

There was no answer, no response, so Avon made sure that the message had been stored and could be repeated. She then encrypted it locally with a simple algorithm so that anyone trying to play it back from the ship would hear nothing but gibberish. She didn't know how long it would go on before the Nihil found it, but when they did, she hoped it would just sound like noise to them. Otherwise someone was going to be in big trouble.

Avon exited the comms room and was preparing to sneak back to Dr. Mkampa's lab when she heard the unmistakable sound of someone clapping. She turned to see Deva, her feathered crest bright even in the gloom of the ship.

"I thought I heard pups scurrying about," she said with a sigh, walking toward Avon with a menacing stride. "You should've just helped Dr. Mkampa make her bombs."

They flew straight to the vice president's house even though it was very late. Vernestra's eyes were gritty, her body aching as it yearned for sleep. But they couldn't rest. Not yet. They were so close to finding out what was happening on Dalna that even if Vernestra had been able to rest, she would've just popped right back up out of bed as soon as she lay down.

Imri landed the shuttle a little ways outside of the city. Vernestra had offered to drop Honesty and Sha'nai back at the temple outpost so they could get some rest. It was still the middle of the night on this part of Dalna. The temple had plenty of extra places to sleep, and they could use the comms in the temple to let their parents know where they were. But it turned out their parents were used to them camping out in the woods as part of their training, ice gators and all, so there were no worries there. And Honesty and Sha'nai were just as anxious as Vernestra to discover what was going on.

So they walked up to the vice president's house as a group, only J-6 staying back to continue her work searching the frequencies for any sign of a message from Avon. The door opened as they approached, and it wasn't the vice president this time but another Theelin man, this one with spotted silver skin and emerald green hair. He saw the boy who walked with them and burst into tears.

"Theo! Oh, come here, my dear son," he exclaimed. The boy, who had refused to speak to anyone but had come along willingly, ran into the man's arms.

"Jedi, thank you for bringing back my son. I'm Hackrack's husband, Zian. You should come in. He's going to want to speak to you."

They filed in behind the man and went into the sitting room he indicated. It was a different room than where they'd met before, and when the vice president entered, he looked frazzled.

"My husband tells me that you've brought back my boy. Where did you find him?" he asked. The strange, smiling man from before was gone, and in his place was a very worried father. Things were not okay on Dalna.

"He was in the Maawat Mountains," Honesty said. "Sir, can you tell us what is going on?"

Hackrack gestured for everyone to sit, so they all made themselves comfortable. When Hackrack sat he was directly across from Vernestra, and he met her eyes with an unwavering gaze. "When you were here before, I lied, which I'm sure you sensed. But you have to believe me that it was for a good reason."

"Why don't you just tell us what's going on," Vernestra said.

Hackrack sighed deeply and then began to talk. "About a week ago, my son, Theo, went missing. He and a group of children were playing in the south meadowlands, and at some point he was just gone. We looked for him, searched high and low, but we couldn't find him. My husband and I returned home, called the security chief, and discovered that we had a message. It was the Nihil. They had taken my son. But that wasn't all. They'd also placed charges on the Bensha Fault, and said that if we tried to find the boy they would detonate the charges. We told the Council and the president, and they advised that we wait to see what it was the Nihil wanted. But they never made any demands other than to leave them be. I'm glad to have my son back, but now I worry what the Nihil will do when they find out."

"Wait, what's the issue with the Bensha Fault?" Imri asked before yawning widely. "Sorry, it's been a long night."

"The entirety of the planet is very unsettled," Lyssa explained. "Dalna is a relatively young planet and up until a few centuries ago was still plagued by frequent ground-quakes and volcanic eruptions. The Bensha Fault is the main space between the tectonic plates. It shifts regularly and runs through the Maawat Mountains."

"It's why we've discouraged settlement in that region," Hackrack said. "The quakes frequently level any dwellings, and there are numerous hot springs that vent volcanic gases. A series of explosions there might set off any number of natural disasters, and that would be terrible."

"If the Nihil kidnapped your son, why is he here on Dalna?" Vernestra asked.

Hackrack shook his head. "I don't know, and that is an excellent question. I'm hoping Theo can tell us."

"Why would the Nihil kidnap your son and set explosives along the fault?" Sha'nai asked. "That seems like too much. One or the other should have been enough to ensure compliance."

Vernestra shook her head. "No, it seems like exactly the sort of thing they would do. The Nihil aren't known for their restraint. If they can't hurt someone they aren't happy."

"So, what now?" Honesty asked.

"Now we sleep," Hackrack said, standing. "We don't know where the charges are, but it'll only be a matter of time until the Nihil find out I have my son back. And then they will think we've betrayed them and try to destroy Dalna."

"Can you evacuate the planet?" Yacek asked.

"Perhaps, but there are nearly one million residents and we have precious few ships here. And I'm not sure my people will leave unless they have to. We Dalnans are not enamored of space travel."

"We can help you," Imri said. "Vernestra and I have fought the Nihil and won."

"Two Jedi cannot protect an entire planet," Hackrack said.

"It wouldn't just be the two of us. We have Yacek and Lyssa and Master Nyla, as well. Plus, we can call for help. Starlight Beacon would be happy to assist."

Hackrack shook his head. "Yesterday someone took out our relay satellite. Most likely the Nihil. I was dealing with that moments before you arrived. Haven't you noticed that you haven't been able to call out while here?"

There was a sudden racket, and they all turned to look at the door, which slid open to reveal J-6.

"Ha! I knew she'd call. You all doubted me, but my logic was sound."

Vernestra blinked. "Jay-Six, what are you talking about?"

"Avon! She sent an emergency announcement. She was kidnapped by the Nihil, and it seems like they're forcing kids to join them or making them work on a farm instead. I don't know which is worse."

Everyone in the room exchanged looks.

"What? Why aren't any of you excited? Isn't that the proper response to long-awaited news?" J-6 asked.

"Yes, but if there are no relay satellites to receive or send messages . . ." Imri began.

"Then maybe the Nihil faked the distress call?" Honesty said. "If they know we've gotten Theo back, it could be a ploy to lure us into responding only to ambush us."

"I know Avon's voice. The distress call matched all two hundred and sixty-three vocal markers," J-6 said.

"Then Avon must have been here on Dalna the entire time," Vernestra said, standing. "It's time to show the Nihil there are consequences for their actions."

SEVENTEEN

Kara Xoo didn't seem very surprised when Deva dragged Avon before her. But she didn't seem amused like she had before, either.

"Aren't you supposed to be using your smarts to help Dr. Mkampa? Disappointing. Deva, I don't suppose you're hungry?"

"Nope, sorry," the woman said, flashing her teeth at Avon. Avon wanted to believe that the woman was joking, but she got the feeling she was not.

"Ah, well, this one is obviously a troublemaker. Chain her. Avon," Kara Xoo said. She rose and descended the stairs from her throne, her face tentacles dancing as she loomed over Avon. "Defying me once is admirable. Twice is foolish. Your life is forfeit. I will not give you the luxury of a third attempt. Take her to the holding pens. We'll deal with her later tomorrow."

Deva hauled Avon backward by the collar of her shirt, and she knew in that moment that she'd made a huge mistake. They were going to kill her, and then what? She'd be dead, and no one would ever design a synthetic kyber crystal that could power any number of things to help the galaxy.

"Wait! Please. I was just looking for something . . . to help Dr. Mkampa. A file I thought you might have in your databank."

Deva and Kara paused. Deva released her, and Avon stumbled as she regained her balance. Both the women watched Avon with a predatory gleam in their eyes. One wrong move and Avon would incur their wrath; she could feel it. One thing that remained true about the Nihil: they loved their violence. Avon had to do all that she could to make sure they didn't suspect she might be lying.

She had so much to live for. This couldn't be her end.

"And what file might that be?" came a new voice.

Avon turned to find Dr. Mkampa walking in. The woman's cold gaze landed on her, but not even a flicker of emotion crossed her face. Avon swallowed dryly. Lying to Kara Xoo and her ilk was one thing, but Dr. Mkampa was a real scientist. She would scent a bit of bantha patty a kilometer away.

"It was Murphis Sewellis's theory on the radiant energy of cross crystal focus, mainly his treatise on integrated kyber crystal structures and the subsequent focusing abilities of a triple-density crystal matrix," Avon said, her heart pounding so loud that it echoed in her ears.

"Absolutely ridiculous," Dr. Mkampa said, and Deva hauled her up once more.

"Deal with her," Kara Xoo said.

Avon didn't get a chance to say anything else. She was dragged roughly from the room and off of the *Poisoned Barb*. Her one chance, wasted on junk science from a junk scientist.

She should've gone with Mian San's theory of shared energy production.

"Well, pup, you should've left well enough alone," Deva said as she clamped a pair of restraints on Avon's wrists. "Dr. Mkampa might be a little ghoulish, but at least you would've had a chance to earn your place among the Nihil working with her. Now Kara is going to sell you to the Zygerrians with the other brats that wouldn't listen."

Avon's fear melted a little. She'd thought they were going to kill her. Being sold into slavery would at least give her a chance at life somewhere else. Right?

The hot tears falling down her cheeks told a different story.

"Wait! Hold on a moment."

Dr. Mkampa came down the boarding ramp behind them, her expression pensive. "Are you saying that Sewellis's theory can be applied to energy systems as long as the overall underlying crystal structure is maintained when applied to arrangement of the larger matrix?"

Avon sniffled once and then again. "Yes, but only if you take into account the work of Mian San and the equal distribution of energy in a crystalline matrix without redundancy," Avon said. She didn't actually think either of those theories would work, whether apart or together. They'd been disproved a number of times. But she wasn't going to give up her future so easily.

"Interesting, very interesting. Hmmm, both of those theories were considered silly and easily disproven three centuries ago, but that was before the advent of Marsabi's focuser. Deva, release her. The girl is brilliant, and I was too hasty."

Deva's thin lips twisted. "Are you sure? Kara won't like it."

"Leave that to me," Dr. Mkampa said. "You are going to help me get my project working. And if you don't, you will meet a particularly terrible fate. Understood?"

"Affirmative," Avon said, her heart in her throat. She had another chance. And she would not waste this one.

She understood what was at stake now. There was no way she would ever make it off of this planet, not the way she was behaving. Vernestra and Imri would have called for help. They would have tried to keep their hopes up, and they would have meditated to maintain their strength.

But Avon was just a regular person. She had more in common with the Nihil than she did with Imri or

Vernestra. If she wanted to survive, she would have to think and behave like the Nihil. By putting herself first.

Avon felt the familiar weight of Imri's kyber crystal in her pocket, and a plan began to form. She would teach these Nihil a lesson. And she would do it by sinking to their level.

It was too late that night to do anything about the message from Avon. J-6 had tried tracing the signal, but with the relay satellite disabled there was no way to get a precise location. Imri and everyone else were exhausted, and they decided to get a few hours of rest before taking their next steps. So Imri flew the *Wishful Thinking* back to the temple outpost, with a promise to bring Honesty and Sha'nai's speeder bikes back the next morning so they could spend a restful night in their own beds.

Once back at the temple, Imri was sure he'd never be able to sleep, but his body had other ideas. He crashed as soon as he laid on the soft sleep pallet, waking to Gemmy kneading him with sharp claws the next morning.

"I get it," he muttered. But then he remembered the events of the night before: finding Theo, learning about the Nihil holding Dalna hostage, and getting the garbled transmission from Avon. J-6 hadn't needed to sleep and was going to work on some ideas about how to find the location of the signal, so Imri bounded up and went to go see if the droid had figured out where Avon might be.

Imri walked into the common area to find it a bustle of activity. Master Nyla, Lyssa, and Yacek conferred in low voices in one corner while a host of Dalnans leaned over a holomap projected above the table. Vernestra caught his eye and waved him over.

"Glad you're awake. You're just in time."

"Did you find Avon?" Imri asked, and Vernestra shook her head.

"No, but the elders think they know where she is. Theo said they took him to a farm at first before deciding he would be better isolated so they could keep a closer eye on him. There's a farm village a few hundred kilometers away, a big one. No one has heard from the families there for some time. The Dalnans have reluctantly agreed to let us go check things out, but the bigger issue right now is the damaged relay. We can't get a message to anyone as long as it's broken, so I was thinking maybe you could go to Starlight Beacon and ask them for help. Master Maru should be able to send along someone to fix the relay and also give us some assistance. We don't have much time. The Dalnans are worried that if we don't find the Nihil quickly, they'll detonate the bombs they planted."

Imri straightened. "I can do that."

Vernestra nodded. "That's what I thought. You can take Lyssa and Hackrack Bep with you. He may have to request Republic aid, and it's better to be certain than take an unnecessary risk. You won't have time to make the trip twice."

Imri realized that Vernestra was trusting him with a huge responsibility. "You think that the Nihil really did plant charges to destroy the planet."

Vernestra's lips thinned into a line, and Imri knew in that moment his mentor was worried. "I do. You've seen what the Nihil are capable of when they set their mind to things."

Imri thought of the Gravity's Heart, an experimental space station the Nihil had built. Vernestra was right. If they could do that, there was no telling what kind of havoc they had planned for Dalna.

"I can leave as soon as the vice president is ready," Imri said.

Vernestra smiled and suddenly pulled Imri into a hug. "I don't know that I've told you this before, but I am so proud of the Jedi you've become. I know you sometimes doubt yourself and your connections with others can be taxing, but I'm really proud of you."

"Vernestra, can you join us? We're going to review the plan," Yacek called. The Mirialan released Imri, and he was surprised to see her eyes shining with pride.

Imri's heart swelled. "Thanks, Vern. That means a lot. Okay, let me get to Starlight so I can hurry back."

"Be careful," Vernestra said. And then she was dashing back to the group of Dalnan officials.

Imri grabbed his few belongings, Gemmy trotting along beside him. Hackrack Bep waited near the *Wishful Thinking*, shifting his weight from foot to foot.

"I dislike space travel," he said, and Imri placed a

calming hand on his arm, smoothing the man's anxiety. The tension immediately drained from Hackrack's posture, and he even gave Imri a bit of a friendly smile.

"Don't worry," Imri said. "I'm an excellent pilot."

NINETEEN

V ernestra tried to keep her eyes open as the president of Dalna, a pale-skinned human woman named Sachary Jeffington, droned on and on about how many locations could not be hiding Nihil because of this reason or another, which was completely a waste of time since they all knew the Nihil had to be somewhere in the Maawat Mountains. At first Vernestra had been excited to meet the president, a farmer wearing homespun clothing who opened the conversation by discussing the upcoming week's weather, but that quickly evaporated when it became clear she was less interested in finding the

Nihil and eliminating them and more concerned about what fighting would do to the gnostra berry plants that were the planet's main source of income.

"I'm still not sure why you can't just talk to these . . . these . . . Who are they again?" she asked.

"The Nihil, sir. They were the ones who hijacked the Coruscant shipments four years ago," said the president's aide, a skinny Toydarian with leathery blue skin and a pronounced snout. He hadn't introduced himself, and the president just referred to him as her aide. The Toydarian flitted around the president, his wings buzzing from the effort of keeping himself aloft, and Vernestra got the feeling that he didn't like it whenever anyone got between him and the woman. She'd tried to keep her distance, but she was beginning to wonder if there was something else afoot.

She thought about what Honesty and Sha'nai had said about the president being elected quite surprisingly and how no one much cared for her. Vernestra could see why. There was something odd about her complete lack of urgency. She had to be stalling.

But why?

"Talking to the Nihil is about as useful as shooting a blaster when it's on safe," said the security chief, Tracer Lore. He was a Vodran with brown skin, pupilless blue eyes, and facial horns. Vernestra hadn't thought Vodran worked for anyone but the Hutts. But that couldn't be true, because there one was, living on Dalna. It just went to show that you couldn't judge people by anything other than their actions.

"I understand that you are hesitant to have Republic Defense troops marching across the land," Vernestra said, "but we have good reason to believe that the Nihil are somewhere in the Maawat Mountains. Perhaps we could take a small scouting party to search likely locations there. Honesty mentioned a village that no one has heard from for a while." She was trying to be diplomatic even though she was anxious to do more than talk. She'd expected this meeting to be productive and quick, a short conversation before they boarded ships and flew over the planet's surface searching for Avon. But it had been nearly two hours of conversation and the most boring discussion of the weather—which was lovely and did not need to be analyzed—that Vernestra had ever endured.

"That doesn't sound like any place I know. Are you sure about that?" the president finally said, stroking her chin in contemplation.

"We should check the Maawat Juncture," Tracer said, meeting Vernestra's gaze and ignoring the president.

"The Maawat Juncture? Where's that?" Yacek asked. He and Master Nyla seemed to be taking the wayward discussions of the Dalnans in stride, and Vernestra could not decide if that was because they'd had more time working with the Dalnans or if it was the result of numerous hours of contemplation. Perhaps their tolerance for frustrating people was just higher than Vernestra's.

"Ahh, the juncture," Sachary said, gesturing toward the map. "It's here, where the Maawat Mountains and the Luftall River come together. Did you know that once upon a time the settlers on Dalna thought this a mystical place? A font of healing or some such? The Veil, some called it. It's actually no such thing, but travelers from all over the galaxy used to journey here to bathe in the waters."

"What's so special about that spot beyond the history?" Master Nyla asked, leaning forward to peer at the map.

"Oh, it's the tip of the Bensha Fault."

"Could charges placed in that area cause a natural disaster?" Master Nyla asked, the older Twi'lek seeming a bit surprised by the idea.

"Yes. And that would be very bad," the president said. "But why would anyone do that?"

"Very, very bad," her aide echoed, his wings flapping a little more in agitation. "But no one will be there."

"We should check it out, anyway," Vernestra said. Something told her that the president and her aide were not to be trusted, and she knew better than to ignore such instincts.

"You have a plan, Jedi?" Tracer said. He also seemed disinclined to buy into the president's nonsense. Honesty said he trusted the man, and Vernestra trusted Honesty.

"Is there a way to fly over and see if there are any Nihil there?" Vernestra asked.

Tracer shook his head. "We aren't spacefaring sorts here on Dalna. There's a supply shuttle that arrives every other week, and you could maybe slip them a few credits to give you a tour?"

"We don't have that kind of time," Vernestra said. She took a deep breath and let it out in an attempt to chase her frustration away. "Is there any other way to get there? How do you usually travel locally on Dalna? Landspeeder? Speeder bikes?"

"Speeder bikes!" the president exclaimed. "Those are entirely too dangerous. Plus, they'd never get up the side of the mountain."

"You could ride a trappu," Tracer said. "It's a large reptile we use to pull our wagons when the landspeeders are busy. The trappu can also sense groundquakes, or at least that's what some of the more remote farmers tell me."

"Trappus are an excellent idea," Master Nyla said.

"Great! How long would it take us to get there on a, uh, trappu?" Vernestra asked.

"Two days. We could find probably ten of them? Leave first thing in the morning," Tracer said. "I'd like to bring my apprentices if you don't mind. You met them, Honesty and Sha'nai?"

"That sounds excellent," Master Nyla said, climbing to her feet. "The day grows late, friends, and if we are taking our leave early in the morning, we're going to have to prepare."

Yacek turned to Master Nyla in surprise. "You're going with us?"

"Yes. I think this is a situation where the outpost being unattended for a short while makes sense. I've had a feeling of unease these past few months, and now I think I understand why."

"We could ask Jay-Six to stay behind," Vernestra offered. "Since Lyssa left with Imri."

Master Nyla frowned. "I suppose that might be a way to ensure that there is someone here to look after things."

Tracer and the rest of the Dalnans stood, as well. "Excellent. We'll see you at first light. Till harvest," he said, turning and leaving with the others.

But not before he had given Vernestra a nod of respect.

Vernestra watched everyone go and had a fine sense of frustration. She took a deep breath and blew it away as best she could. Taking their time and approaching the problem in a rational manner was the best course of action. She had to remember that.

But it was difficult when she thought of Avon there among the Nihil, trying to survive. Were they torturing her? Had she eaten? It was uncomfortable to be so focused on a single emotion, to worry so much about another person, but Vernestra couldn't help herself. This wasn't the all-consuming focus of attachment that the Order so often warned Padawans about. Avon was her friend, and more than that, she had once been Vernestra's charge. She still felt a measure of responsibility for the girl.

Vernestra would feel the same way if something were to happen to Imri. It was only natural to worry and care about others, but she had to be mindful it did not dominate her thoughts.

She took another deep breath and released it. She would meditate and rest. When it was time to fight for Avon's freedom—and Vernestra had no doubt there would be a fight—she would be ready.

TWENTY

Imri stood in Jedi Master Avar Kriss's office on Starlight Beacon and tried not to squirm. Being so close to the Jedi Master was always a little unnerving for Imri. Not because she was mean or scary, but because she was cool and collected even in the midst of most disasters. Imri had once joked that if Starlight Beacon were to be hit by a comet, Avar wouldn't even sigh about it.

That was not the Jedi he had found that morning. After nearly a day's flight, Imri had been rumpled and tired. But Master Avar looked even worse. She was agitated and restless, like she hadn't slept well in a while. When

Master Maru had explained why Imri and Hackrack Bep were in the office, Lyssa using the trip to take advantage of Starlight's impressive databank, Avar's usually calm expression had twisted into one of surprise and then outrage.

"Why didn't we know they took out the communications relay in the Dalnan system?" Avar asked. "What about the one near Haileap? Is the relay still active there?"

"I have asked Rodor Keen and his Republic engineers to run a diagnostic," Master Maru said. "From our end it looks like the relays are working just fine, so I'm not sure what the issue could be. I've sent a team out to check the Dalnan satellite in person. We should know the problem by early tomorrow."

"And what of the rumored threat to Dalna? And the Nihil?"

"I have asked the Republic to send an envoy to assist," said a dark-skinned human woman who had just entered the room. Her hair was piled on top of her head, the braids intricately woven together, and the woman's perfume tickled Imri's nose. "If my Avon is there, I will use the full force of my position to ensure that these Nihil do no harm to my daughter."

Imri blinked as he took in the woman. It was Senator Ghirra Starros, Avon's mother. Imri had met her briefly a short time before, on Coruscant, but apparently the woman didn't remember him, as she hadn't bothered to greet him. But it could be because she had other things on her mind. Her daughter was missing, and Imri didn't need to reach out to her to sense the waves of panic and fear emanating from her.

Avar nodded and sighed. "Thank you, Senator. Estala, get me a report on those relays as soon as possible. Imri, why don't you take Vice President Bep to secure some quarters. I need to call the Council. If the Nihil have gone to ground on Dalna, then this might be our best chance to end things with them once and for all."

"Agreed. And the sooner I can get my daughter back, the sooner I can return to my duties on Coruscant," Senator Starros said.

Imri nodded, taking the direction as dismissal. He escorted the vice president to a suite set aside for visiting dignitaries—there were several, but it was good luck that one was empty, since they rarely were—before going to his own quarters and taking a shower and changing his clothing. The loaner tunic and trousers from Dalna had been nice at the time, but there was something comforting about wearing his own clothes.

Imri had just lain down and was beginning to drift when he startled awake. He couldn't have said why, but for some reason he had the strongest sense he should go find Vice President Bep. Hackrack had been nervous their entire trip, but Imri had chalked that up to the man leaving Dalna for the first time. Imri remembered how nervous Honesty had been even before the disaster on the *Steady Wing*, mostly because Dalnans didn't travel much. But this had seemed different. Like something more.

Imri dragged himself from his bed with a sigh. He didn't like to attribute everything to the Force, but there was no mistaking the *pull* he felt. This was more than just his subconscious trying to remind him of something he'd forgotten.

Something was wrong.

Imri headed for the quarters where he'd left Hackrack and knocked gently on the door. He waited, listening intently. There was no sound from the other side, and he was reluctant to open the door uninvited. It had been a long trip from Dalna; it could be that the vice president was resting.

Pain. Fear. Surprise.

Imri had just turned away from the door to Hackrack's suite when the emotions cut through his mind. And now he could feel it: a deep sense of foreboding. He tried the door mechanism, but the door refused to budge.

Imri drew his lightsaber and powered it up, the blade glowing palest blue in the corridor.

"Vice President Bep! I'm coming in!" Imri said. He cut through the door locking mechanism with his lightsaber and then held his hand up to the door and used the Force to open it fully. The vice president was sprawled on the floor, unconscious, and the rapidly swelling lump on his head made it clear that someone had hurt him. Imri holstered his lightsaber and went to the intercom in the wall to call for medical help.

There wasn't much amiss in the room. Everything was in its place, but Imri wasn't the person to figure out what had gone wrong. There were cams everywhere on Starlight.

Not in the room where Hackrack lay, but everywhere else. Someone had entered and hurt the man. They would find out what happened.

A strange scent tickled Imri's nose. Perfume. He tried to identify the scent, but it was too light to really be sure. Imri thought it smelled a lot like Senator Starros. Had she come to visit Hackrack after Imri had led him to his room?

It was possible, but only a small part of the mystery. Imri wondered why someone had hurt the Dalnan vice president. Surely there couldn't be Nihil on Starlight Beacon?

The thought was too ridiculous to even consider.

TWENTY-ONE

A von had told herself that the best way to stop Dr. Mkampa was to become the woman's best asset. Professor Kip had once said that a good assistant was as important to progress as the right tools, and Avon had decided to become just that.

It was easier than she'd thought.

The first day after her trip to the comms room, Dr. Mkampa had kept Avon chained by the ankle to the worktable, giving her just enough distance to travel among the various machines. Avon had figured it would be a permanent arrangement, but then Dr. Mkampa had suddenly unfastened the ankle cuff right after the midday meal.

"This is ridiculous. No great mind can work at its fullest potential when it is encumbered by restraints," she said. Avon knew it was a test. So she thanked the doctor and went back to her assigned task, which was duplicating the pile of crystals into larger constructs. Avon waited until Dr. Mkampa left before pulling Imri's kyber crystal from her pocket and using the crystal analyzer to map its shape. Then, after making a few alterations to the basic structure, Avon began to replicate the thing as much as she could. It was impossible to fully replicate a kyber crystal. The matrix itself was too complex, and it was thought by many powerful scientists that the crystals could even shift their shape depending on ambient energies, one of the reasons only the Jedi could use them with any real efficacy, but Avon did the best she could in a ramshackle lab full of old machines. The result was a crystal that focused energy perfectly but was highly unstable, prone to shattering after any kind of sustained energy refraction.

It was perfect. And Dr. Mkampa did not seem to notice the switch.

That day passed, and by the second day in the lab, Dr. Mkampa no longer stared at Avon when she thought the girl wasn't watching. And Avon kept making flawed kyber reproductions. That was the problem with any kind of copy crystal: they were highly unstable. A Jedi with a replica kyber crystal might find their lightsaber suddenly exploding, and no scientist would ever endorse such a move. But Avon wasn't trying to help Dr. Mkampa. She was trying to stop her from ever hurting anyone else again.

Avon kept expecting Dr. Mkampa to analyze one of the reproductions and see the flaw that Avon had put in the design. And when the woman rested a heavy hand on Avon's shoulder, Avon half expected she had discovered just that. Instead, the doctor announced that they were going to go check on something a small distance away.

"I'd like for you to accompany me to check on the progress of my project," Dr. Mkampa said with a chilly smile. "I think you should see what your work has accomplished."

Avon didn't say anything. She'd been practicing the tight-lipped emotionless thing the Jedi were known for since the last time she'd been with Vernestra, who was pretty good at it. It was harder than it looked, but Avon had discovered that many people felt it was necessary to fill the silence with their own words, and that had been invaluable with Dr. Mkampa. In the past few days she'd told Avon more about the Nihil than anyone else, even Royce.

"I had a whole factory, you know. A delightful factory where I created the fog of war, and a few other surprises, as well. And now I have this," Dr. Mkampa said, gesturing to the workbench where Avon tried to avoid putting together too many gas bombs. "Abysmal. Soon you'll see just how much the Nihil can provide when properly motivated. This is a new chapter. I very much believe that. The Jedi will lose interest, and then life can be good again." She'd been trying to commiserate with Avon, but instead she'd brightened the girl's day. That night Avon had fallen asleep hoping that the Jedi would burst into the camp at any given moment.

But instead she'd woken to an instant bun and a bottle of sweetdrink. J-6 never would've let her have so much sweetdrink, and the thought had brought fresh tears to Avon's eyes.

Avon had once longed for adventure, and now she regretted it. She just wanted to go home.

Dr. Mkampa led the way out of the camp. They had to walk down a dusty, narrow track that looked more suited to wild animals than any kind of biped. Avon had a moment when she considered pushing the woman ahead of her down a steep hill, but then she realized that wouldn't solve any of her problems. Dr. Mkampa was more cybernetic than she was human, and it would be Avon's rotten luck that the woman would bounce right back up.

No, if Avon wanted to best Dr. Mkampa, she would have to do it by outsmarting her. She had already set foot down that road, so she just needed to stay the course.

The trail they were on suddenly widened, depositing them alongside a metallic-smelling river. The water was rust red, and Avon hoped that whatever was about to happen, they wouldn't have to get near it.

But Dr. Mkampa turned back toward a row of metallic obelisks that had been installed next to the river. The ground had been hollowed out, and Avon's first question was, how had someone implanted the objects way out in the middle of nowhere?

"This, Avon Sunvale, is my crowning achievement. Each of these towers contains a crystal matrix that I've harmonized to the underlying structure of the planet. I believe that the tectonic plates in any planet function just like any other crystal in a systemically linked matrix, and with the proper alignment of energy I can manipulate them as I wish."

"Are you talking about making a groundquake machine?" Avon said, horrified at the towers before her.

"Something like that. I'm thinking more of the possible terraforming applications." Dr. Mkampa was lying. Avon could tell by the way she smiled at the menacing spires, even going so far as to stroke one. This woman might love science as much as Avon, but they were nothing alike. Avon wanted to use science to help the galaxy. Dr. Mkampa seemed to just love destruction. "With your help I've finally puzzled out what I was missing, and so you are now going to help me test them out. Shall we?"

Avon said nothing, just watched as the woman opened a panel in the side of the nearest spire. A row of glowing crystals lit the inside, and Avon was surprised to see they looked like kyber crystals. They were *her* crystals, rows and rows of the crystals Avon had been making, all with that singular flaw. Dr. Mkampa took a cracked crystal out and replaced it with one of the synthetic crystals Avon had created the day before.

Immediately the network began to glow, and there was a curious sensation as the land around them started to tremble. Dr. Mkampa laughed, the sound ominous. Avon steadied herself by placing a hand on a nearby tree and watched as Dr. Mkampa pulled out the crystal to power down the machine.

"Avon Sunvale, you are a genius, my girl," Dr. Mkampa said with a grin. "Completing this matrix using the combined principles of both Sewellis and San was not something I would've expected to work, but it does. Utterly brilliant."

Avon pressed her lips together. It shouldn't have worked! Especially not with the flawed crystals she'd given the doctor. But Avon couldn't let her know that. Instead, she forced a smile.

"I'm glad I could be of help. I . . . Can I ask a favor, Dr. Mkampa?"

"What? Yes, of course! Anything, dear child. You have utterly changed my life today."

"The kids I came here with, the ones that were, uh, going away to become part of a Strike. Could I possibly see them? I just want to know how they are." Avon's brain was taking this new information and modifying the plan that had been brewing since the night Kara Xoo had threatened her life.

"What? Why would you want to see them? They're nowhere near your level."

Avon forced a laugh. "I know. But they mocked me when I tried to explain Kemp's theory of conservation to them, so I want to make sure they know how great things are going for me now."

Dr. Mkampa smiled and nodded. "That is a brilliant reason. Let me see what I can do. Let's head back. I have the feeling that Kara Xoo is going to want to thank you personally when she finds out what you've done."

Avon doubted that, but she would do anything to get a chance to talk to Krylind, Liam, and Petri once more.

After all, if she was going to destroy the Nihil, she would need help.

TWENTY-TWO

They were halfway through the day's ride when the groundquake struck. The trappu Vernestra rode, which looked to her like a skinnier dewback with a wicked beak, reared up suddenly, letting out a hoarse scream. A few seconds later, rocks began to slide down the hill, and the world itself became unstable.

"Quake!" Yacek called from up ahead, where he rode a trappu of his own. A boulder came sliding down the hill toward them, and Vernestra held on to the reins with her right hand while using the Force to catch the boulder with her left, grunting at the effort of pausing its advance. She pushed it to the side, clear of the narrow track they rode along.

"Strange," Tracer grunted. "This is not the ground-quake season."

"Groundquakes have seasons?" Vernestra asked, patting the side of her trappu to help settle the beast. After a few moments they continued their progress up the side of the mountain.

"Everything has a season," Tracer said, and that seemed to be the end of that.

The group fell silent as they continued on their way. Vernestra couldn't help thinking how much faster it would have been to fly to the place instead of riding beasts of burden, but Imri had not yet returned and the Dalnans had been adamant that trappus were the only way to get to the Maawat Juncture. Vernestra could see how that was the truth as they rode the beasts down a narrow, winding track. To their left was the mountainside. On the right the land fell away into a sheer cliff face. If Vernestra were nervous about heights, she would've been anxious riding along the dusty trail, but she was mostly wondering what was going on with Imri and Avon. Were they both safe?

Had Imri made it to Starlight and let them know about the issues on Dalna? Vernestra had to believe that both were exactly as they should be. That was all she could do.

There was also the matter of the president and her strange behavior. Vernestra had wanted to get Tracer alone to discuss the woman's caginess. It was suspicious that she didn't seem to want to make sure the Nihil weren't camped out somewhere on the planet, but Vernestra got the feeling that the security chief was avoiding her. She wondered if that was because he didn't like Jedi or he didn't want to accidentally say something that would get him in trouble. No matter. The issue would be resolved one way or the other when they got to their destination.

She had to trust in the Force that everything would work out for the best.

They'd only gone a bit farther when the trail widened out into a small grassy meadow. Tracer called a halt from his place in the front, and as he dismounted his trappu, everyone else did the same.

"There's another hard climb, and then we'll be at the Maawat Juncture," the security chief said. "We should let the trappus graze for a while and take a break of our own for the night. It'll be dark soon, and it's a bad idea to try to push too far. These mountains can be very dangerous."

Everyone nodded in agreement, and Vernestra stretched, her muscles tight and knotted after so much time on the unfamiliar animal. She was about to reach into her pack for something to eat when movement in the trees grabbed her attention. Vernestra drew her lightsaber at the same time a grubby figure burst from the woods, headed right for Master Nyla. The older Jedi held an instant bun in one hand, and the dirt-covered human boy, who was no more than ten or eleven, had his hands out, reaching for the food.

Master Nyla raised a hand, using the Force to lift the boy into the air in front of her before he could snatch her meal. The boy made a squealing sound of despair, and Vernestra searched the trees for anyone else. The boy seemed to be alone, so she holstered her lightsaber.

"Is he okay?" Honesty asked. He and Sha'nai had kept to themselves most of the trip, as though the presence of Master Nyla discomfited them a bit.

"I believe the child is just hungry," Master Nyla said, handing the boy her bun before setting him on the ground.

The boy snatched the food and shoved it into his mouth, whimpering as he did so.

"Where could he have come from?" Sha'nai wondered aloud.

"Up there, most likely," Yacek said, pointing to a nearby mountain.

"Do you have a name, little one?" Master Nyla asked the boy, handing him a canteen so he would have something to wash his food down with.

"It's Liam," he said after swallowing. "Are you a Jedi?" Master Nyla nodded. "I am."

"Are you here to save Avon? And maybe the rest of us?" he asked.

"You know Avon?" Honesty said, and the younger boy took another bite, nodding as he chewed.

"She said the Jedi were going to save us," he said around a mouthful of bun. "But I heard that Kara Xoo had Deva eat her."

Vernestra frowned. Kara Xoo was the name she'd heard in her hyperspace vision. "Who are Kara Xoo and Deva?" she asked. She was trying not to let her excitement show. The boy knew of Avon, which meant she had to still be alive. Plus, Vernestra felt like she would know if Avon were gone, the same way she'd known the exact moment Douglas Sunvale had died. Avon was too bright of a light for her to become part of the cosmic Force without a ripple.

"Kara Xoo is a Tempest Runner, and Deva is her friend. They're mean," he said. There was so much the boy wasn't telling them, but his expression said it all. He was terrified of Kara and Deva.

"Let's let Liam eat in peace. We can ask him more questions after he's finished his food," Master Nyla said. Vernestra wanted to argue, but the older Jedi was right. The boy had obviously been through some trauma. What he needed was a moment to gather himself.

But Vernestra knew everything she needed to know. If Avon was nearby, she would find her. She just had to remind herself that patience was what would win the day.

Even if she wanted to charge back the way the boy had come and find her friend.

Vernestra took a deep breath and let out a sigh. Sometimes she wished she could be irrational, but that went against every single bit of her training.

Being a Jedi was hard.

TWENTY-THREE

Imri paced outside of Starlight Beacon's command hub and tried to be calm. That was what Vernestra would do. "Tranquility, Imri! All will be revealed in its time," she would say, the admonishment so frequent that Imri could hear his master's voice clearly in his mind. But Imri had the feeling that they were quickly running out of time, and not just for Avon but for something much, much bigger. Even if he didn't have words for it.

Starlight's doctor, the snakelike Dr. Gino'le, had told Imri that he'd been just in time to save the vice president. "He has a very serious head injury, and if you hadn't checked on him, he might not have lived. It looks like someone hit him with something heavy, but not sure what it could be." That had sent Ghal Tarpfen and Velko Jahen, two Republic officials, off to look for the culprit. With all the cams on Starlight Beacon, it should have been easy to find out who had attacked the vice president.

But there they were a day later with nothing. It was a curious thing, and Imri could sense that this was a matter worth investigating. Not just because someone had gotten hurt—although that was reason enough—but because there was something bigger here.

Imri and Lyssa, who had been just as shocked to hear of the vice president's condition as everyone else, met with Velko Jahen in Starlight's dining area. The Soikan woman, with her silvery skin and hair, was upset when they found her sitting at a table that overlooked one of Starlight's many gardens. Waves of worry and confusion washed over Imri, and he instinctively rested his hand on her arm to ease some of her distress.

"Administrator Velko, have you found anything about who might have entered Vice President Hackrack's room?" Imri asked.

The Republic official shook her head. "No. There's no sign of anyone entering his room, and it looks like the images from that cam have somehow been corrupted. I think"—and here Velko lowered her voice, giving both Imri and Lyssa an odd look—"I think you should speak to Maru. Because there is something strange going on here."

"Like what?" Lyssa asked.

"Like someone purposely turning off the other cams in that hallway. I don't have the clearances to check the command logs, otherwise I'd tell you who did it."

There was a beeping from Velko's uniform, and she pulled a comlink from her pocket. "Velko Jahen."

"Administrator," Master Maru said, "there's a matter that needs your attention. Come to the command hub immediately."

Velko put the comlink away and tilted her head toward the door. "I have a feeling this is about our injured vice president. You should come with me."

Imri didn't need to be asked twice. He, Lyssa, and Velko made their way to the turbolift and then to the command hub, their pace only slightly less than a run.

When they arrived the door slid open and they entered.

The command hub was mostly empty, but Master Maru sat in the midst of a number of screens, some of them showing the interior of Starlight Beacon, some feeding from other parts of the galaxy.

"Master Maru?" Imri called.

"Padawan! How are you? And Jedi Lyssa. I suppose you are looking for an update on the communications relay in the Dalnan system. Or not. Administrator Velko," Maru said with a somber look. "I suppose this is about another matter entirely."

"Yes, Master Maru," Lyssa said.

"It's about the injuries sustained by Vice President Bep."

"Ah. How is the vice president?" Master Maru asked.

"Resting," Imri said.

"Velko told us that the cams were completely turned off by someone with a higher-level clearance than hers," Lyssa said.

"Yes. The security chief, Ghal Tarpfen. Which is why I called Velko, but I suppose you should hear this, as well. We've been looking for her, because I have some questions, but she seems to have fled Starlight."

"What?" Imri said, not able to keep his outburst to himself. "What do you mean?"

"I'm afraid it looks as though she might have been behind the attack on Hackrack. We aren't sure why, and with Ghal on the run, I have more questions than answers. I was hoping Velko could help with that," Master Maru replied, stroking his chin.

Velko held up her hands. "I had no idea Ghal was even gone from Starlight. We just had the early meal together. When did she go missing?"

"Near as I can figure, about an hour ago," Master Maru said.

"I have to talk to Rodor Keen, since he is the Republic official in charge of Starlight Beacon and needs to know what is happening. But don't worry, Master Maru, we'll find her." Velko gave them all a quick nod of respect and then took her leave, heading off to pursue her own duties.

"Do you think she was Nihil?" Lyssa asked after Velko had gone, crossing her arms. "Have the space pirates really managed to infiltrate the Republic that way?"

"I don't know," Maru said. "But I worry that without

the answers to those questions, we will never fully defeat the Nihil."

There was a long pause, the silence heavy with all the things the Jedi were thinking. Imri thought about all the people who had been lost to the violence of the Nihil— in the Great Disaster, not to mention the attack on Valo. The Nihil would never stop, not unless the Jedi could stop them first, and Imri couldn't help sighing.

"What about the relay?" he asked.

Master Maru gestured them forward.

"The teams reported in a few minutes ago, so your timing is quite good. The relay to the Dalnan system was damaged, although it would be hard to say whether that was the result of regular space debris or whether it was intentional. Any calls coming from Dalna should be received now."

"Has there been anything?" Imri asked.

Maru shook his head. "No, not yet. But Vernestra will call if she needs assistance."

"What about the Republic troops?" Lyssa said. "Imri said Senator Starros was going to ensure that they sent someone to assist."

Maru frowned. "That is an excellent question. I haven't heard anything, and my calls have gone unanswered for the moment. But Senator Starros has been an asset in battling the Nihil, so I am sure it is just a matter of rallying the peacekeepers."

"What do we do? Should we head back to Dalna?" Imri asked. "Vernestra wanted me to bring reinforcements, but we don't even know if the Nihil really are on Dalna."

"No, and I've sent a message to the temple on Dalna but I haven't gotten any sort of response. For now, we need to get organized so that we are ready to respond when Dalna calls for assistance. Perhaps you should try speaking with the vice president when he wakes," Maru said, stroking his furred chin as he thought. "I know he is not a naturally trusting sort, but you could soothe his reservations and perhaps get a measure of truth from the man. I have the feeling he is the key piece to this puzzle."

Imri nodded. "I will. Thanks." He and Lyssa took their leave, the older Jedi heading back to the archives to do more research on both Dalna and its volcano system and Imri making his way to the medcenter. As he walked, Imri made a mental list of questions for the vice president. He considered Master Maru's words. "Soothe his reservations," he'd said.

Was Master Maru urging Imri to use his abilities to question the man?

Imri didn't know, and when he returned to the med-center, it was only to be told by one of the med techs that the man was sleeping. But that was no matter. Imri found a comfortable spot to sit and began to wait once more, beginning one of the meditations Vernestra had taught him.

He would find out what was going on, even if it required an ocean of patience.

TWENTY-FOUR

Avon was a bit surprised when Dr. Mkampa let her see the other kids from the *Poisoned Barb*. The meeting was held in the Nihil mess hall, a room that smelled like spoiled food and had a disconcerting number of stains on the dirt floor. There were about fifty kids in the hall, sitting pressed close together, eyes downcast, shoulders hunched as though they were anticipating a blow at any moment.

"See what you saved yourself from?" Dr. Mkampa said with a wave at the space. "Your brilliance lifted you out of this kind of obscurity. Most of these fools will die on the wrong end of a blaster, their lives spent in meaningless violence. But you will endure, just as I have." Dr. Mkampa squeezed Avon's shoulder. Avon thought maybe it was meant to be comforting, but it was just painful, and she had to work to hide her wince. "You have a quarter of an hour, and then we must return to our work."

Avon walked between the rows of tables, looking for Petri, Krylind, and Liam. All the kids had a similar look about them, hopeless and dirty, and Avon could feel them staring at her. She'd had daily visits to the shower, and Dr. Mkampa had been adamant about finding her a decent change of clothes. Even though the woman was bad, she had taken good care of Avon, and that gave the girl a strange feeling. Should she be grateful to Dr. Mkampa? Why should Avon worry about the woman wanting to kill people when she'd taken such great care of Avon?

It was a discomfiting line of thought, so Avon turned her attention somewhere else: back to her reason for finding the other kids.

She finally spotted Krylind's pale green skin at the far end of a table. Avon squeezed in next to the girl, who looked at her in alarm before she realized it was Avon.

"Stars, I can't believe you're still here. And alive!" Krylind said.

"I am. Where are Petri and Liam?" Avon asked. She still hadn't seen either of the boys.

Krylind shrugged. "I don't know. Petri was sitting with the recruits last time I saw, the kids who get to graduate to better things. He said he wasn't going to end up a drudge, working on some farm. Squib taught him how to use a blaster, and he kept getting in fights, so Yeet took him with them on a Strike run. I haven't seen Liam since he ran off."

"He escaped?" Avon said. She had looked at the terrain, estimated her chances of escape, and decided that rescue was the better option. Now she wondered if she'd misjudged.

"He had to," Krylind said, her eyes darting around to make sure none of the Nihil were paying attention. Avon saw them near the door, laughing over some joke. "He stole some food the second night we were here. They tried to chase him, but he ran off. I thought maybe he went to find you, but you're here and he's not."

"I hope he got away," Avon said.

"Me too," Krylind said. "Look, I don't know what you

want, but I can't help you. I'm scared, and they watch us all the time. Did you know they sell anyone they don't like to the Zygerrians? I don't want to be enslaved," Krylind said, sniffling a little.

"You don't have to. I have a plan. And all you have to do is run to the *Poisoned Barb* when the groundquakes start."

"Groundquakes," Krylind said, looking up with wide eyes. "Was that you? Yesterday?"

"Maybe. Look, it's going to be confusing when things start happening, so make sure everyone runs on board the ship, okay? That's it."

"I can try, but I don't know that anyone will listen to me," she said, sort of folding into herself. Footsteps approached behind Avon, and Krylind suddenly ducked her head once more. Avon turned around to find Dr. Mkampa standing behind her.

"Have you had enough?" the woman asked, her voice chilly.

"Yes," Avon said, standing. She hoped she looked properly haughty, like she was enjoying rubbing her good fortune in the faces of others. "Thank you."

They took their leave, and as they passed the group of Nihil standing near the door, Avon pretended she'd just had a great idea. "It's really too bad we can't show everyone else how brilliant your machine is," she said.

Dr. Mkampa didn't say anything, but Avon went ahead and continued talking, as if she were talking to herself. "You're more powerful than any of them, and yet they have no idea of your genius."

"How exactly would we plan a demonstration?" Dr. Mkampa said with a laugh. "The obelisks work because they've been embedded deep enough to tickle a fault. There isn't nearly enough space there to gather a crowd."

Avon said nothing. This was where she would let Dr. Mkampa figure it out herself.

She had her own plans to untangle.

"And that's everything I know," Liam said, finishing his story for the second time. The first time he'd told the assembled group about his harrowing experience being kidnapped by the Nihil, they'd tried not to interrupt the boy, and after that everyone had decided to find their rest for the night. But the next morning over breakfast they'd asked the boy to tell them everything he knew once more, bombarding him with questions about not only the Nihil but the other children he'd met in the Nihil training camp. The more they asked the boy, the less clear it all became.

But there was no doubt: the Nihil had been kidnapping children and had brought them to Dalna, where the officials were too scared to disturb them much. It made Vernestra wonder how many other places were sheltering the Nihil out of fear.

Once Liam was fed and had shared all that he knew about the encampment, it was decided that he should return to the city with Honesty and Sha'nai. Tracer's apprentices knew the way back, and it would also be a chance for them to call Starlight and Imri for an update, if they could get through. Vernestra had no idea how long it would take to get the relays repaired.

"Waste no time returning," Tracer said as he saw the trio off. "We're going to need help."

"Go to the temple and use that comm," Vernestra said. "It might be easier than going to the president. You can call Starlight directly. Jay-Six can help you if necessary."

Tracer grunted in agreement, and Vernestra figured that was confirmation that he didn't trust the president all that much, either.

"We'll hurry," Honesty said. "And be careful."

Vernestra simply clapped the boy on the shoulder. She

had no answer for him. She would do what was necessary to free the children the Nihil had stolen. That was all there was to it.

After the departure of the apprentices and the boy, Master Nyla pulled the rest of them aside.

"If this is a Tempest, that is entirely too many Nihil for us to take on directly," she said. "And I worry that taking the trappus any closer will alert the Nihil to our presence."

"That is a good instinct," Tracer said. "Perhaps we should continue on foot."

"And then what?" Yacek said. "What do we do once we get there? Just wait and watch?"

"No," Master Nyla said. "We think of a way to liberate as many of the children as possible without fighting."

"Let's not make a decision just yet," Vernestra said. "One of the things I've learned about the Nihil is that their plans are always evolving. We might get there and find only a handful of them. But we should consolidate our packs and get going."

That was one point they could all agree on, so they removed the packs from the trappus, left the animals to graze in the clearing, and began to take a more direct path to the Nihil encampment following the directions Liam had given them.

Hold on, Avon. I'm coming, Vernestra thought.

She just hoped they wouldn't be too late.

TWENTY-SIX

After she spoke with Krylind, a feeling of excitement lodged in Avon's belly. She didn't know why, because she was only returning to the lab to do the same work. But somehow she just knew it was going to be a pretty good day.

After the midday meal she returned from the refresher to find the lab full. At least twenty Nihil, including Kara Xoo and Deva, were crowded into the small space. They huddled around a plate of crystals, and Dr. Mkampa was lecturing them about the process of crystal modification and polarization.

"Avon! Good, you're back. Would you like to explain to Kara and Deva how the crystal matrix engineering process works?" Dr. Mkampa said.

Avon swallowed thickly. "Um, I think you already did? It's mostly about making sure the crystals work in a series to increase the magnification. It's easier to show than to explain," she said. Avon tried not to look at the crystals on the workbench. She had stayed up late the night before to make a more efficient batch, or at least that was what she'd told Dr. Mkampa. The reality was that the crystals were the most deeply flawed ones yet. Avon had realized after the demonstration with the obelisks that the crystals she was creating weren't flawed enough. She couldn't wait for the crystals to fail. They needed to fail immediately, and spectacularly. So Avon had created the newest batch to have deep flaws by making sure the matrices were unstable. The only problem was that she hadn't yet gotten the chance to test the failure rate of the crystals. Avon had no idea how bad it would be if they used her newest batch. But whatever happened, it would be explosive; that was for sure.

"Avon is right," Dr. Mkampa said. "Kara, I humbly

request that we adjourn to the epicenter, where I've set up my obelisks."

Kara Xoo's face tentacles danced, but she crossed her arms and gave a short shake of her head. "No, not yet. There will be time for that, but this is not the moment. The Dalnans have left us to our own devices, and attacking them right now before we are ready to move on would be silly."

"Dalna?" Avon said, even though no one was paying her any mind. She knew people on Dalna! They weren't even all that far from Haileap.

Liam had been right to run away. Now Avon only wished she'd run away sooner instead of waiting.

"You might change your tune when you hear what I have to say," a Toydarian wearing a full face mask said, hovering near the door. "The communications relay has been restored, and Hackrack Bep is on Starlight Beacon asking for assistance. It's only a matter of time before the Jedi are here."

Kara Xoo growled. "Why was I not notified of this sooner?"

"I just got the information from my cousin," said the Toydarian, his leathery hands held up in surrender. "Sachary and her aide have already retreated back to No-Space. It seems she got nervous when the Jedi began to press her and made her exit ahead of schedule."

"That coward," Kara growled.

The Toydarian ducked his head. "I said the same thing, my Tempest. I came to find you as soon as I heard."

Kara Xoo nodded, then she thrust her fist into the air. "Let's show these Dalnans the might of the Nihil! It's time to leave, friends. Sachary may be a disappointment, but she has lived longer than most Nihil because of it. But before we go, we're going to need to resupply. So let's have some fun. Saludad is ripe for the picking."

The group began to whoop and filed out of the lab. Avon watched them go, only the cold hand of Dr. Mkampa bringing her back to the moment.

"Leave those fools to their mischief. We have work to do," Dr. Mkampa said. There was a strange expression on her face, something between disappointment and frustration, and Avon gave the woman a sad smile.

"I'm sorry they don't care about your genius. A few well-timed quakes could be far scarier than a bunch of gas and looting."

Dr. Mkampa's lips thinned, and she moved away. "You're right. This constant dismissal is beginning to chafe."

"Maybe we should ready the machines anyway? Just in case Kara changes her mind?" Avon offered. "If we create a series of groundquakes while the rest of the Nihil are looting, that could really show the might of the, um, Tempest?" Avon offered. As soon as they powered up the machines with that new batch of crystals, there would be instant disaster. With most of the Nihil gone, off to pillage the nearby towns and villages, the chances of escape improved for her and all the rest of the kids who had been kidnapped.

"Maybe . . . You continue to synthesize a few more of those Sunvale crystals," the doctor said with a smile, as though giving Avon that miniscule bit of acknowledgment meant something, "and I will go and check out the current status of the machine."

Dr. Mkampa scooped up a handful of the new crystals—the crystals in her matrix regularly burned themselves out because of the power involved—and walked out.

Avon paced for a moment. What was she going to do? If she couldn't convince Dr. Mkampa to turn on her machine at full power, there would be no distraction for her and the other kids to flee. Turning the machine on at full power would definitely create an explosion, and Avon was counting on that to give them a chance to overpower the Nihil, at least the ones who remained as the rest prepared to leave Dalna.

The roar of ships launching dragged Avon from her despair spiral. She went to the lab door and watched the Nihil leaving. They flew off toward the Dalnan capital city.

The Dalnans would have no idea what was coming.

Avon knew in that moment that this was her chance. There would not be another opportunity to sabotage Dr. Mkampa's machine, and there would never be better odds. With many of the Nihil gone, Avon had less risk of being detected as she went through the camp.

Avon walked out of the lab, moving with a sense of purpose. She was deciding whether to go toward Dr. Mkampa's machine or toward the building where they kept the kids locked up when there was an explosion. There was a single loud boom, then another, and Avon couldn't help smiling.

It sounded like Dr. Mkampa had decided to install the new crystals in her machine after all. And judging from the explosions and the smoke in the sky, she had gone for full power.

Avon didn't wait to see what happened next. She ran toward the building where most of the kids were kept. The Nihil standing guard in front of the doors raised their blasters at her.

"Hold it right there, brat, before we blast ya," said a Quarren man with a blotchy brown face, his tentacles dancing in agitation.

"We need to run! Dr. Mkampa's machine just exploded. Do you know what's going to happen next?" Avon asked. She didn't think the man would buy it, but then the world seemed to tilt precipitously to the left and again to the right. That was when Avon realized she'd miscalculated. The machine had exploded, just as she had wanted. But not before sending a pulse down to the fault line.

The quake seemed to go on and on. Buildings rattled as pieces of them fell to the ground. Avon took a deep breath and threw herself into the Quarren man, using the quake as a distraction. The man tried to shove her back, but Avon managed to get her fingers under the pull pin on one of the canisters hanging from the bandolier across his body.

"Sorry!" she said, leaping backward, trying to escape the gas that suddenly surrounded them. Avon scurried backward from the gas while the two Nihil fumbled for their masks. They were unsuccessful, and the blue gas billowed around them until they fell to the ground, unconscious.

The ground calmed, the quake ending abruptly. Avon waited at a safe distance until the canister finished belching its toxic contents, and then she grabbed the keys from the Quarren man's waistband and used it to unlock the door to where the kids were kept.

When she opened the door, all she could see beyond were shadows. "Hey! It's me, Avon! Come on, we have to get out of here."

"Clever, very clever," came a voice behind Avon. She turned to see Dr. Mkampa standing behind her, half of her body singed like she had been set on fire. With some of her clothing burned away, the circuits below were fully revealed. "I should have checked those crystals. That is what I get for not assuming you could be as devious as the rest of us. Well done."

Avon took a step backward as the doctor stalked toward her. She looked around for something to do, some way to escape. Her eyes landed on the blaster still holstered at the Quarren man's waist. But just as she lunged for it, Dr. Mkampa launched herself at Avon, picking her up and throwing her against the building.

Every nerve in Avon's body screamed as she slammed into the metal wall. The doctor's cold gaze chilled Avon as she gasped for breath. She was going to die.

"Avon! Stay down!"

Avon crouched against the side of the building as Vernestra Rwoh launched herself through the air, the familiar purple blade of her lightsaber a welcome sight. Dr. Mkampa turned to face this new threat, and Vernestra slashed her lightsaber down toward the woman. But Dr. Mkampa was quick and leapt out of the way.

"Jedi," Dr. Mkampa said, the word sounding like an insult.

Vernestra held a hand up, throwing the woman backward into the far-off tree line with the Force.

That should have been the end of it, but no sooner had Vernestra turned back to Avon than Dr. Mkampa came running full tilt toward Vernestra. She grabbed the Mirialan's tabard and held her aloft, eyes glowing red like hot coals.

"You have your tricks, but I have science on my side," Dr. Mkampa said, throwing Vernestra so she slammed into a nearby tree. At first Avon was afraid that was the final blow. But the Jedi hit the tree and ricocheted off, her lightsaber held out in front of her as she slashed downward at Dr. Mkampa again.

"The Force, you mean?" Vernestra said, landing nimbly and kicking out at Dr. Mkampa. The woman easily dodged the kick and twisted off her hand to reveal a blaster barrel where her wrist had been.

Avon did not think that was an ethical body modification, but she was fascinated by it.

Vernestra did a backflip out of the way of the sudden blaster fire from Dr. Mkampa's arm. As the Jedi moved, she twisted the bezel on her lightsaber and the blade melted into a whip, the sinuous purple plasma blade still deadly. When she landed on her feet once more, she flipped the whip at Dr. Mkampa's wrist. The tip of the light whip caught hold of the metal, melting it and sealing the barrel shut.

"Fascinating," Dr. Mkampa said, studying the melted metal of her wrist but making no more threatening moves toward Vernestra, who seemed to be waiting for the next attack. Dr. Mkampa's lips twisted in a terrifying smile. "Until next time, Jedi." And then she turned and ran into the forest, moving far faster than any human Avon had ever seen.

Vernestra made no move to chase her, and in a matter of seconds the highly augmented woman had disappeared into the woods.

"She's getting away," Avon said, finding the escape deeply unfair.

"We have other matters to attend to," Vernestra said, holstering her lightsaber. "Such as saving you."

Hot tears prickled Avon's eyes, and she sniffed. "It's about time. You're at least a day past my calculations."

"I'm glad you're safe, as well, Avon," Vernestra said, wrapping her up in a hug. The Mirialan smelled of sweat and some other strange, musty odor. But Avon didn't mind. She was just happy to be rescued.

"Where were the Nihil headed to?" Vernestra asked.

"To Saludad, they said. They heard that the Dalnans

had betrayed them, so they wanted to teach them a quick lesson. If we hurry we can get everyone out of here before they return."

"We should warn the city," Vernestra said, waving over one of the other Jedi who was with her, a pale human man with dark hair. After a quick, low-voiced conversation he rushed off. "And good idea. It was truly nice of them to leave us a ship. You get everyone on board, and the other Jedi and I will take care of the remaining Nihil. It's good to see you safe and sound, Avon."

Vernestra ran off, and Avon ran back over to the doorway.

"You heard the Jedi!" she yelled to the kids huddled in the gloom. They began to stand, a few coming forward so the sunlight caught their hopeful expressions. "Let's go!"

Vernestra ran through the camp, opening doors to buildings and pens, hustling kids of all ages and species to the lone Nihil ship docked not too far away. It was a medium-sized ship, and there were more kids than Vernestra had imagined, but they would get all of them away from the Nihil. Even if it was a tight fit.

When the massive groundquake had struck, Vernestra and the rest of her group had seen it as the perfect moment to attack. They'd watched the Nihil fly away a bit earlier, but the quake had seemed like an omen.

Master Nyla and Yacek had freed most of the kids,

as well as at least five families who shied away from the Jedi until they saw Tracer. The handful of Nihil who had been left behind had been subdued, many of them bound with their own restraints. Vernestra and the other Jedi had done one last run-through of all the buildings to make sure there was no one left behind. The ground was beginning to tremble again.

"All of these quakes are a bad omen," Tracer said, scratching his wide chin. "This is starting to feel like volcano season."

"There's a volcano season?" Yacek asked, but before Tracer could answer, he held up his hand. "No, you know what? Never mind. I don't want to know."

"The groundquakes are caused by a crystalline power matrix that Dr. Mkampa tied into the planet's crust," Avon said. "I don't think we should—" Whatever she was about to say was cut off as a particularly large tremor sent her flying into Vernestra, who steadied the younger girl despite the instability of the planet. "Never mind. That one was definitely stronger."

"Look!" Master Nyla said, pointing toward the trees. There was a plume of red smoke rising into the air, and a few seconds later the ground began to shake again.

"Dr. Mkampa must have found a way to restart her machine," Avon said with a frown. "We have to stop her."

"You have to get out of here," Vernestra said, pointing toward the lone shuttle as she drew her lightsaber once more. "It's going to be crowded, but you go with the rest of the kids back to the temple. Jay-Six is waiting there for you. Yacek and I will take care of the doctor. Once and for all."

"Yes. To the temple," Tracer said. "We can send a message to the protection forces in Saludad on our way there. They did not respond to our last message, and I have some concerns."

"Wait, what is that?" Yacek said, pointing to a red haze coming from the nearby trees.

"The forest is on fire!" Avon said.

Vernestra holstered her lightsaber. "I suppose that means we should all flee together."

"Definitely. Those flames are moving quickly, and last time I checked, I wasn't flameproof. We need to get out of here," Yacek said.

The villainous doctor might have escaped, but they had still accomplished their mission for the time being. The families huddled on board the small skiff, its miniscule size most likely why the Nihil had left it behind. Vernestra and Yacek hurried aboard the Nihil ship, which looked like it had once been a planet jumper, running short routes between nearby planets. The thing didn't even look to have any kind of a hyperdrive. Luckily the interior was empty, the cargo hold large enough to accommodate all the children and the missing families, and Vernestra watched as a few of them hugged one another, reunited after weeks apart. Vernestra wondered how many other kids had been forced to work with the Nihil throughout the Outer Rim. It was one more reason the Nihil had to be stopped, and quickly.

She tried to ignore the strange feeling that perhaps the Nihil were more resilient than the Jedi and the Republic knew. It seemed like the Nihil were recruiting any way they could, and Vernestra knew there had to be abducted children who were even now proud members of the Nihil.

How could they stop an organization that was always growing, always finding new members—even by force?

Yacek walked straight to the cockpit, and as the ship lifted off, Vernestra took a deep breath and let it out. She'd accomplished her mission, and she felt like she could finally relax.

"Oh, no! Look."

Avon had taken the copilot's seat, Master Nyla happily relinquishing it. Avon pointed down to the trees that surrounded the Nihil encampment, and at first Vernestra wasn't sure what was the matter; they already knew there was a fire.

But the forest wasn't just aflame. A sinuous river of glowing red wound its way through the trees.

"What is that?" Vernestra said, leaning over Avon to peer out the cockpit's front viewport.

"Lava, I think," Master Nyla said, crossing her arms. "It seems as though the Nihil really did have a plan, after all."

❦

When the hauler touched down in front of the temple, Vernestra got right to work, helping assign the children and families to rooms and finding them pallets to rest on. There were about a hundred people in all, but most of them were children, the youngest one gripping a doll, the eldest crossing her arms as though she wanted to defy the Jedi.

"I'm going to go put a big pot of stew on," Yacek said. "We're going to have a lot of hungry people." He disappeared soon after, as though the sight of so many children made him nervous. Or perhaps he was thinking of the disaster it would be when the kids were all hungry.

J-6 came out of the temple at a near run, sliding to a stop before Avon. "You are in so much trouble! I was very worried, and my circuits are not programmed for such things, so you can imagine how hard it was for me," the droid said. "Are you unharmed?"

"Yes, Jay-Six. And I missed you, too," she said, patting the droid awkwardly. "But now we need to get everyone settled. Will you help me?"

"My primary programming is for childcare, so I would say I am well-equipped for such a thing. But you promise never to make me worry about you again."

"I promise," Avon said with a smile, and Vernestra tried not to consider the idea that droids could learn to have emotions. It was a bit too weird.

"Okay, listen up," Avon said to the kids milling about, not even giving Vernestra or Master Nyla a chance to address the group. "The Jedi are here to help. But that means we have to help them. Everyone grab a pallet. Big kids help the little ones. Once you have a sleep pallet, find an empty room. We're going to have to sleep together, one big happy family. If you don't get a pallet, don't worry. We'll find you one. And hey, help each other out. We've all been through something awful. That's not an excuse to be a jerk."

"Avon," Vernestra began, but her heart wasn't in it. She was just glad to have her friend back, safe and sound.

"Don't worry, Vern. I know you've been busy. We're going to help," Avon said with a small smile. Vernestra could feel that there was something Avon was avoiding thinking about, but she didn't get a chance to ask her what was going on before the girl took off to help Master Nyla hand out supplies, J-6 following along and a few of the other adults that they'd just rescued pitching in, as well.

Tracer headed out once he was certain that everything was being handled. He was going to borrow the temple's landspeeder and promised he would return with extra supplies. Vernestra was just about to believe that everything was settled when Yacek entered the common room.

"Vern, I think you should hear this," he said.

Vernestra wrinkled her nose at the nickname but followed the older Jedi Knight to the storeroom where they kept the comm unit. There was a distress call playing through the speakers.

"If you can hear this, please help. This is the Dalnan Council. The volcanic system on Dalna has been activated, and we need to evacuate. This is an emergency, and every Republic official and Jedi who receives this is asked to respond."

"Is this true?" Vernestra asked, unsure about the message.

"If it isn't," Yacek said, "I'm not sure why anyone would send such a message. I reached out to Saludad and I haven't gotten any response from the government."

"Avon said the Nihil were headed there, but they may have decided to hit a few other outposts, as well. Have you sent another warning to the Dalnan outposts?"

"I did, but I'll send it again. You should head with Tracer to Saludad, if he hasn't already left. I'll see if I can reach Starlight Beacon and request assistance from them directly."

Vernestra nodded and ran out to see if she could still catch a ride with Tracer to the capital city.

TWENTY-EIGHT

Imri was still waiting for Vice President Hackrack Bep to wake up when Lyssa found him sitting in the medcenter.

"Any news?"

Imri shook his head, and Lyssa filled him in on the call for help and said Starlight was discussing a response.

"How do you know all of this?" Imri asked.

"Librarians are notorious gossips, if you didn't know. Anyway, I came to find you and Hackrack, because if anyone can give the Jedi a good idea of what needs to be done, it's him," Lyssa said. "I think this is what Master Maru meant by us needing to speak to the vice president. Not just about who might have attacked him, but also about the issue with the groundquakes and the volcanoes. Starlight is formulating a response, and a few ships have already left to help evacuate the smaller cities, but perhaps Hackrack knows just what kind of assistance is needed."

"What about the Republic peacekeepers who were supposed to head to Dalna?" Imri asked.

"Senator Starros says she is still working on it, but it will be days before the Republic can respond," Lyssa said.

"Really?" Imri asked. That seemed strange to him. During the Great Disaster the Republic had been able to mobilize in hours. "So it's up to us."

At that moment, Dr. Gino'le came out of the rear of the medcenter, waving one of his prosthetic arms at Imri.

"Mr. Bep is awake now. He says he'd like to talk to you," the Anacondan said, his sinuous body turning back the way he'd come as soon as he'd delivered his message.

"Let's go see what he has to say," Lyssa said, leading the way toward the vice president's room. Imri followed, and when they entered they found Hackrack propped up against some pillows, a medical droid handing him a glass of juice.

"Padawan Imri. And Jedi Knight Lyssa. How are you, my friends?" the Theelin said, his expression a bit dazed.

"Vice President. How are you feeling?" Imri asked while Lyssa shooed the med droid from the room.

"Good, thanks to you. I heard that I have you to thank for saving my life."

Imri shrugged. "I'm just glad I was in time. Look, sir, I have to ask you something, and it's very important. Do you know who attacked you?"

He shook his head. "No. When I entered my room, the lights were out, and I just remember a feeling of pain and not much after that."

"Do you know the security chief here on Starlight? Ghal Tarpfen? She's a Mon Calamari."

"I've never heard of her. You think she attacked me?"

"She fled after you were hurt," Lyssa said. "And it seems like she turned off the cams in the hallway leading to your room."

"I'm sorry," Hackrack said, shaking his head. "I've never heard that name before."

"What can you tell us about groundquakes and volcanic eruptions on Dalna?" Imri asked.

Hackrack sighed. "Oh, no. It's just as I feared. Has there been some major disaster?"

"Starlight Beacon received a call for help, saying that the entire planet had become unstable. Do you have any idea how big of a problem this could be? Should the planet be evacuated?" Lyssa asked.

"Yes, most definitely, especially if this was caused by the Nihil, and it sounds like it may have been. The day my son went missing, there was some strange seismic activity in the Maawat Mountains. We monitor all of the seismic activity on Dalna. Groundquakes are a given, but a few years ago a geologist was called in to discover why the crops kept dying in a particular valley. It was discovered that the planet's crust was incredibly thin in that area. Most planetary crusts are hundreds of kilometers deep. In that valley, there was less than a hundred kilometers between the surface and the planet's magma layer. The toxic gases were venting all the time, killing the crops and making the people sick. If that was where the charges were placed, it would create a chain reaction of groundquakes followed by volcanic eruptions followed by more groundquakes, and so on and so forth. In a week the entire planet would be uninhabitable."

"We need to tell Master Maru all of this," Imri said.

"Yes. Dalna will have to be evacuated, like Jedi Lyssa suggested. The geologist we consulted said that prolonged instability in the region could lead to disaster. The quakes could lead to volcanic eruptions, which create toxic gases and lava flows. But how will we get everyone off the planet? There are a million people. And it would take a very long time to organize ships to help evacuate, if any even heeded the call for assistance."

"We'll talk to Master Maru," Imri said. "You rest."

He turned and left, Lyssa following along behind.

"How will we organize that many ships to save the people of Dalna?" Lyssa wondered aloud. "It's too bad we can't just bring Starlight Beacon to them."

"Maybe we can. . . ." Imri said, his voice trailing off. "It makes the most sense. It's big enough that a lot of people could be brought here until they find new places to live, or until the planet can be stabilized. It's not a permanent solution, but it's a good one for now."

Imri began to jog, and Lyssa kept up with him as he ran full tilt toward Starlight Beacon's command center.

He just hoped that Starlight Beacon could save Dalna before it was too late.

TWENTY-NINE

The trip back to Saludad was short. Tracer drove the landspeeder at top speed, the engine smoking just a bit as they got to the outskirts of the city. They arrived to find the city smoldering, and Vernestra's heart sank. They were too late.

A few of the houses on the outskirts looked as though they had been set aflame, and people were out and about, many of them looking upset and a few crying. Debris littered the streets, and the crops outside the town had a scorched look to them.

"Nihil," Tracer said. "This is no good."

The most noticeable difference was the house that had belonged to the vice president. It was a smoldering ruin, completely destroyed, and as they sped by, Vernestra was relieved to see Hackrack's husband and son unharmed, standing before the wreck and holding each other. The Nihil had attacked, but it looked like they hadn't done much more than destroy the homes of a few people.

"We should find the Council and discover what happened to the president," Tracer said. "She should have sent that alert, and since she didn't, things might be worse than we know."

They made their way through the city to the president's house, which was next door to the Council chambers. But when they knocked, first on the president's door and then on the Council chambers entrance, no one answered.

"You won't find anyone there," called a human woman, sweeping up a few broken bits of pottery. "She ran off with the Nihil, her and that aide of hers. I knew she was shady, but to think she was Nihil the whole time . . ." The woman's voice trailed off, and she shook her head.

"What about the Council?" Vernestra asked.

"Fled, every last one. Bunch of cowards. They were probably being paid off by the Nihil, as well."

"So if everyone's gone, who sent the request for emergency aid?" Vernestra asked.

"I did," Honesty said, running up with Sha'nai. "We decided to come back to the city rather than stay at the Jedi temple after we left Liam there. The security office has an emergency alert system, and as soon as the sensors in the Maawat Juncture went off, we sent the alert. We haven't gotten any answer back, though."

Tracer grunted. "Let's go to the security office and see what we can figure out. Those sensors were put in place to monitor the juncture for dangerous activity."

"I suppose lava would meet that criteria?" Vernestra said.

Tracer nodded. "Things are going to get very bad, very quickly."

Tracer and Vernestra hurried to the security office with Honesty and Sha'nai. A large table with a holomap of Dalna dominated the space, and there were several flashing lights on the map that looked very, very bad.

"What are those?" Vernestra asked.

"The yellow ones are the epicenters of groundquakes. The red are places where dormant volcanoes are showing more activity," Tracer said. As he spoke the ground began to shake, and Honesty and Sha'nai grabbed for the edge of the table to steady themselves. Vernestra used the Force to keep her footing, and as she watched, a new pinpoint of yellow bloomed on the map.

"How bad is it?" she asked, looking at the holo.

"In about two weeks the entirety of the planet will be covered in lava," Tracer said. "Maybe sooner."

"We should evacuate everyone to the emergency shelter on Hansibel Island," Honesty said. "We can use the comms there to continue to call for help, and with everyone in one place it'll be easier to evacuate the planet."

"Plus, it's surrounded by the Bragh Ocean," Sha'nai said. "That has to buy us some time."

"Yes, but the lava won't be our main problem," Tracer said, stroking his chin. "The toxic gases will be. Either way, we'll keep sounding the evacuation alert and activate the emergency corps. That way, we can coordinate and make sure everyone is alerted, even those without comm units."

"How many people can your emergency shelter hold?" Vernestra asked.

"Comfortably? A few hundred thousand. We'll just have to make it work," Tracer said.

"I'll head back to the temple and let them know we need to move," Vernestra said. "Yacek and Master Nyla will be happy to help. The temple should have some supplies we can use, as well."

She dashed back to the landspeeder, her mind running through the possibilities. There were so many people on Dalna. How would they manage to save all of them? The Nihil had created a disaster to cover their escape. How many more people would die before the pirates were stopped?

Vernestra shook her head, clearing away the thought. That wasn't the problem just now. She had to worry more about where they would put all the people fleeing the lava. Even though the emergency shelter was on a large island, it wouldn't take long before it was full. The important thing would be to get everyone off of Dalna and somewhere safe.

One thing at a time, Vernestra thought. She would focus on getting back to the temple and getting the children and the families situated on the island, and worry about everything else later.

It was the only thing she could do.

CHAPTER THIRTY

Imri and Lyssa ran to Avar Kriss's office, not willing to waste any more time waiting to talk to the Jedi Master since she was the marshal of Starlight and most likely to be in charge of the response to Dalna's tragedy. They arrived to find a gathering of Republic officials and Jedi, everyone deciding how best to help Dalna.

Imri and Lyssa hesitated on the threshold, but not for long. Master Maru saw them and waved them in, causing Velko Jahen, the Republic administrator they'd spoken to earlier, to hesitate in her speech.

"Imri. Lyssa. You have something," Master Avar said.

"We do. We spoke to the vice president of Dalna, Hackrack Bep, and he believes that once the volcanoes start erupting, the planet is a lost cause," Lyssa said. "He confirmed what we all suspected."

"But I have an idea," Imri said, his palms slicking with sweat as he spoke. So many important people were in that room, it was hard not to be a little nervous.

Tranquility, Imri, came Vernestra's voice in his mind. Not her actual voice, but the memory of so many lessons and so much time spent together. *Through serenity comes strength.*

Imri took a deep, cleansing breath, and blew it out before he continued. Everyone watched him expectantly. "We should take Starlight to Dalna."

There was a moment of stunned silence, and Imri felt the need to fill it. "I read that Starlight was built with hyperspace abilities because Chancellor Soh wanted to have Starlight go on a galaxy-wide tour, so I thought maybe we could ask for permission to move it now. You know. To help."

He was rambling, so Imri bit his lip. It was a silly idea, maybe, but there were a lot of people on Dalna, and if things got as bad as the vice president said they would, it was going to take too long to evacuate everyone. To Imri, it sounded like a good solution.

Rodor Keen, a human man with pale skin and bushy eyebrows, stroked his chin as his cybernetic eye flashed. "That's actually a very good idea. However, we haven't brought the hyperspace engines online just yet."

"Why aren't the hyperspace engines functional?" Avar asked.

Rodor sighed. "Administrative obstacles, I'm afraid. We've been waiting for a few final pieces, and the Republic delayed sending them because they were too busy dealing with the Nihil."

"What about a tandem jump?" Lyssa said.

"What is that?" asked Master Maru.

"It's a process that used to be done long ago, before every ship had a hyperspace drive. Basically, each ship would engage their tractor beam on the other, and the ship with the hyperdrive would jump, pulling the other one along with it."

Rodor Keen shook his head. "The energy required to lock a tractor beam onto Starlight and also pull the station would be astronomical. But you might be on to something. We can generate a hyperspace field. With tow cables attached to a few other ships, we could gain enough speed to actually make the jump. But there's only a single Longbeam here at Starlight at the moment, and I'm not certain how many others are close by. We would need a few incredibly large ships to make such a jump."

"What about the *Halcyon*?" Master Maru said. He set his datapad on a nearby table, projecting a hologram of a large star cruiser. "It should be arriving momentarily as part of one of its current frontier tours."

"That's a pleasure cruiser, not a hauler," Administrator Velko Jahen said, a frown crinkling her silver skin. "How can that help?"

"It has more than enough power," said Rodor with a grin. "The *Halcyon* is a *Purgill*-class with thirteen engines. With that, the Longbeam, and perhaps a few of the larger haulers, we should be able to get Starlight through hyperspace to Dalna," Rodor said. "Senator Starros said she called for help from the Republic, but they are occupied with a situation near Hon-Tallos. So I'm thinking we're going to be on our own."

"I have the contact information for every hauler currently on Starlight," Velko said, standing. "We should speak to them, quickly, to organize the jump."

"Good idea. I'll go down to talk to engineering while Velko reaches out to the captains of the larger haulers," Rodor Keen said. "I'll also let the Chancellor's office know that we are responding to the issue on Dalna."

"Imri, Lyssa," Avar said. "Why don't you help oversee the attachment of the tow cables?"

Imri and Lyssa nodded, and then they were off.

It didn't take long to get the ship captains on Starlight to agree to help. Most of them thought the idea was risky, but the chance for an adventure was its own reward. A few other captains were reluctant to be part of such a potentially dangerous maneuver. After all, if something went wrong with the tow cables, Starlight could be left to disintegrate in hyperspace, or the station could suddenly end up halfway across the galaxy in the wrong direction. But most of those captains were eventually convinced by the idea of helping Dalna.

There were only a few who outright refused, citing tight schedules. Velko informed those captains that they would want to vacate Starlight before the jump happened, and not another moment was wasted on them.

Imri found himself assigned to the *Halcyon* to attach the cables from the star cruiser back to Starlight. The last time Imri had been aboard a star cruiser, it had been destroyed by the Nihil, so he was a bit nervous as he arrived to meet the captain, a very tall Kel Dor man with orange leathery skin who wore a mask and goggles, his gray-and-blue *Halcyon* uniform crisp and tailored as he met Imri on the bridge.

"Jedi. Welcome. I am Captain Gol Ponk. Do you have any questions for me before we get to work?"

Imri shifted in the strange suit he wore, specially designed for such things as space walks, and shook his head. "No, Captain. I just need to sync my comlink with yours and then I can get to work!"

Imri followed the captain through gleaming corridors and grand dining rooms filled with guests of all species, to the *Halcyon*'s docking bay, where hundreds of kilometers of steelton lay coiled on the deck. He looked past the atmospheric shields to the lights of Starlight, and he began to chuckle to himself.

Seemed like Vernestra's jumping lessons were about to come in handy.

The work required concentration and the Force, for no human could lift the steelton chain when the ship's gravity pulled against it. Imri used the Force to lift the end of the heavy metal chain, pulling it beyond the atmospheric shield in conjunction with four droids and a Wookiee mechanic who barked orders in Shyriiwook. Once outside of the shield, the chain was weightless, the magnets in the bottom of the suit the only thing keeping Imri from drifting off into space.

Imri connected the smaller anchor chain attached to the steelton chain to his waist before using the Force to propel each footfall as he ran to the exposed lip of the ship's bay, leaping when he reached the edge and pushing off explosively. The momentum took him sailing quickly through the emptiness of space, and when he looked around he saw dozens of other Jedi doing the same thing. He was pretty sure he even saw Master Maru flying through space, a steelton chain raveling out behind him.

Imri felt light and happy as he worked, the other Starlight Jedi working alongside him. Vernestra had once told him that a Jedi was at their best when they were helping others. "The closest we ever come to being truly one with the Force is when we're working to help make the galaxy a better place for everyone."

In that moment Imri knew that Vernestra was right, and he was proud to be able to call himself a Jedi.

✦

By the next morning—Rodor having given all the cargo vessels that wanted to leave time to depart—dozens of haulers, skippers, and other ships of various sizes surrounded Starlight Beacon, their steelton cables occasionally glinting in the darkness of space. The pleasure cruiser *Halcyon* was by far the largest ship, and it took the point position, glimmering in the near distance.

Imri and Lyssa stood on the observation deck nearest to the Jedi wing with a number of other Jedi and watched the ships beyond the clear barrier. Some still wore their vac suits, and the chatter was muted as people considered the undertaking before them. For once there was nothing a Jedi could really do but watch. The entire success of the operation was up to Rodor Keen and the captains flying their various ships.

"Do you think it'll work?" an Ithorian Jedi Imri had never seen before asked with the mechanical voice of a translator, his wide flat head and bulbous eyes swiveling this way and that.

"If it doesn't we'll never know," another joked, this one a stocky, dark-skinned human woman wearing mission attire.

Next to him, Lyssa's nervousness rolled off of her in waves. Imri patted her hand, soothing her a bit. "Don't worry. It'll work."

"I know. It's just, if it doesn't . . . I should've stressed the risks of a tandem jump, maybe. Although this is a bit different," Lyssa said, and Imri shrugged.

"All of those ship captains know what they're doing. We just have to trust in the Force and know that all will work out for the best."

The group of Jedi fell silent after that, and for a long

moment there was nothing. And then, outside of the view-port, the afterburners of dozens of ships began to glow as each ship cycled up for a jump. Imri held his breath.

The ships winked out of existence, all at once, their timing synchronized. For a moment nothing happened, Imri's pulse loud in his ears. And then there was a strange feeling of tipping, like Imri had suddenly lost his balance. But before he could correct or even move, he was steady on his feet once more and the blue of hyperspace streamed past the window.

"It worked!" Lyssa said, and the Jedi on the observation deck cheered, jumping up and down in excitement. Imri just smiled, his heart feeling incredibly full. Outside of the viewport the ships had reappeared, maintaining their positions even in hyperspace. Imri had never seen another ship outside of a viewport within hyperspace, and he knew that they had accomplished something quite impressive.

But he couldn't really celebrate just yet.

"Don't worry, Vern," he said under his breath. "We're on our way."

CHAPTER THIRTY-ONE

The next few days passed in a blur for Vernestra. With the Nihil gone, there was not a single sign of the marauders after the attack on Saludad, and the temple outpost and the emergency corps began to work together to evacuate everyone quickly and safely to Hansibel Island. There were only a handful of landspeeders, and the main task was to ferry people from the mainland to the island quickly before the lava overran the majority of the continent.

The day after the groundquakes began, the first of the volcanoes in the Maawat Mountains erupted. The sight was visible even from the temple outpost, ash and dirt shooting into the air kilometers away. By the second day, two more volcanoes had erupted, and the normally blue-green sky became a dingy gray. Respirators were given to those helping alert the most distant homesteads to evacuate, but they were hard pressed to keep up with the rapidly deteriorating air quality. People began to have raspy coughs that echoed strangely as they breathed, and the buildings on Hansibel Island were outfitted with filtration systems cobbled together from whatever could be found, Avon helping make sure the systems ran efficiently.

And still more and more volcanoes erupted.

On the third day after the first volcanic eruption, the temperature on Dalna increased several degrees. The temperate planet had become unbearably hot. The buildings on Hansibel Island were crowded and the uncomfortable temperature made tempers short. Fights broke out, people who had lost everything arguing with one another over ration packs or sleeping spaces. The constant onslaught of emotions made Vernestra's head pound and soured her stomach so that eating was an impossibility, and she was glad that Imri wasn't there to experience it.

Vernestra found Honesty later that afternoon, sitting and staring off into the distance. She had expected to find the same upset and horror from him as the rest of the Dalnans, but instead he seemed calm. "Honesty. Well met."

He turned to smile at her. "Well met, Vern."

"You seem . . . calm. I'm sorry your home has been destroyed."

Honesty laughed, the sound bitter. "It hasn't really been home since my father died. He always wanted to leave Dalna, always wanted to see more of the galaxy. But his duties kept him here. So I'm not really sad the planet has to be evacuated. I'm sure the scientists will come in after we leave, stabilize things, and in a few years most everyone will return." Honesty shook his head. "But I won't. Sha'nai and I have discussed it, and we're thinking about going to join the protection forces somewhere else. Maybe with the San Tekkas. I hear they're always hiring."

Vernestra blinked, a bit taken aback by the conversation. "Oh. I see."

"But even so, I'm not sure you'll hear this from anyone else: thank you. To you and the rest of the Jedi for all that you've done. And if there's ever anything else I can do for you, ever, just let me know."

After her impromptu heart-to-heart conversation with Honesty, Vernestra found herself wondering how many other Dalnans saw the situation as not an end but a potential start of something better. She hoped it was more than just Honesty and Sha'nai.

The next day things had begun to look even grimmer, the lava rolling into the seawater, steam marking where it entered the ocean in the distance, when a glimmer of hope appeared in the sky.

Vernestra was trying to meditate on a patch of grass outside, despite the poor air quality, and kept finding herself pulled back to the moment by one distracting thought or another. She had all but given up when Avon came running to find her.

"Vern! We're saved. Starlight Beacon is here."

Vernestra wasn't sure what Avon meant, but then the girl handed her the macrobinoculars she held. When Vernestra raised the device to her eyes, she could see it: there, glimmering in the sky just past the ash that clogged the air and burned lungs, was none other than Starlight Beacon being towed by a number of much smaller ships, all of them working together to bring relief to Dalna.

"I think that's the *Halcyon* in front," Avon said as Vernestra handed the macrobinoculars back. "I've heard they have an interesting hyperdrive arrangement and I hope we get a chance to take a tour."

Trust Avon to be more interested in the mechanics of a ship than her own rescue.

"Does everyone know that the station has arrived?" Vernestra asked, just as people began to pour out of the emergency shelters scattered around the island.

"We're saved!" came a far-off shout, followed by a chorus of cheers. Avon smiled.

"I think they know," she said, running off.

Vernestra remained where she sat in the grass and just watched the scene unfold around her. People who had been bickering and crying and mourning the loss of their planet now cheered and hugged one another, and a light feeling passed through Vernestra, the weight of the past few days finally lifting from her.

Vernestra smiled. "Good job, Imri," she said, because she had no doubt it was her Padawan who had helped make sure just such a thing happened.

The rescue progressed rather quickly after that. Starlight Beacon coordinated a series of shuttles, and people were ferried from the shelters on Hansibel Island to Starlight Beacon, the Jedi and Republic officials working quickly to get people off the planet. It still took nearly two days to get everyone to safety.

Vernestra and the other Jedi waited until everyone else had departed before finding themselves spots on one of the last transports, Avon and J-6 coming along with them. As they flew, the droid plugged in to recharge, leaving Avon and Vernestra alone in their tiny corner of the ship. The girl was quiet, and Vernestra patted her lightly on the hand.

"None of this is your fault, Avon," she said, and the girl shook her head.

"It is though. The crystals that Dr. Mkampa used for her machine? They were based off of this," Avon pulled a crystal from her pocket, and Vernestra didn't recognize it at first. "This is from Imri's lightsaber. I took it after it got broken on Wevo. I think maybe . . . maybe I shouldn't have it. I understand now what you used to say about how there are some things that aren't for me. I think this is one of them."

"Oh, Avon," she said. She didn't have words to make the girl feel better, to soothe the maelstrom of emotions she could sense within her. That was work Avon would have to do herself. "Hold on to it, and give it back to Imri when we get to Starlight Beacon. He's going to be excited to see you, and I think this is something you should tell him yourself."

Avon nodded and slipped the kyber back into her pocket. The rest of the short ride passed in silence, each of them deep within their own thoughts.

Once the shuttle had docked and they had given their names to the droid keeping track of everyone so people could later find their loved ones, Avon and Vernestra bypassed the Republic officials handing out room assignments and made their way to the main concourse. They'd barely stepped off the lift to the floor where the Jedi stayed when Vernestra was engulfed in a hug.

"Vern! You made it!" Imri said, lifting her up a bit

before putting her back down. J-6 stood nearby, muttering to herself about organics and their penchant for emotion. He then turned to Avon, and his joyous expression melted away.

"Avon, what's wrong?" he said.

"Can we talk?" Avon said before bursting into tears.

"Of course! Hey, what's wrong?" Imri asked. Vernestra moved away to give the two some privacy.

If Avon needed someone to talk to, there was no one better than Imri.

THIRTY-TWO

Avon never liked apologizing, but when she handed Imri his kyber crystal and told him about everything that had happened—being kidnapped, how she had used his crystal to help Dr. Mkampa, and all the other sordid details—she found that she immediately felt better.

Too good, in fact.

"Hey, are you using the Force?" Avon asked, and Imri shrugged guiltily.

"You were so upset, I just wanted to help a bit," he said.

"You should not be helping Avon after she stole

something important from you. You should be relishing her pain," J-6 said.

"Can we get a little privacy?" Avon huffed at the droid.

"Fine, I need to oil these joints, anyway."

J-6 moved away, walking toward the droid supply area, and Avon turned back to Imri.

"Jay-Six is right. You should be mad, not trying to make me feel better! I stole your broken lightsaber," Avon said, a fresh wave of tears about to overtake her.

"Avon," Imri said, his voice gentle and the hand he put on her shoulder warm and friendly. "I already knew."

Avon blinked and sniffed a bit. "You did?"

"Of course. Where else could it have gotten to?"

"So why didn't you ever ask for it back?"

Imri sighed and shrugged. "I guess I figured that it was in good hands? You're the smartest person I've ever met, Avon. If anyone could figure out how to use a kyber for more than just lightsabers, some kind of thing that could help lots of people, it would be you."

That just made Avon feel like crying all over again. Imri patted her on the shoulder. "I'm not mad, and we're good. Don't worry about it. Hey, do you want to tour the

Halcyon with me? The captain said I was welcome to take a look around the ship before it leaves tomorrow."

Avon nodded but didn't get a chance to say much more, because a familiar scent tickled her nose, followed by a shout on the concourse.

"Avon!" yelled Senator Starros as she hurried past awestruck Dalnan refugees and a contingent of Jedi handing out room assignments and ration packs. "Thank the stars. I was so worried!"

Avon was gathered up in a fierce hug, and she was so overwhelmed with emotions, she could only pat her mother's back awkwardly. "Hello, Mother. Sorry I made you come all the way to Starlight."

"Nonsense. We were due for a visit, anyway. I'm just glad that horrible Quarren Kara Xoo and her people didn't hurt you. Especially that Deva and Dr. Mkampa. You're lucky we found you when we did."

Avon didn't say anything, just let her mother continue talking until she'd said her piece. When the senator released her, Avon gave her mother a tremulous smile.

"Mother, I'm glad to be here, but I have to debrief the Jedi right now. And then Imri and I are going to take a tour of the *Halcyon*. Why don't I meet you at the dining area for the evening meal so I can change into something a bit more presentable?"

"Oh, good idea. And make sure you tell the Jedi everything that happened. The sooner they can take care of these Nihil, the sooner you can get back to your studies."

Avon nodded before turning to Imri. "We can go now."

As they moved off down the concourse, Imri gave Avon an odd look. "Avon, you could have stayed with your mother. What's wrong?"

"Do you know who Dr. Mkampa is?" Avon asked.

"No, why?"

"She was the one who built the weapon that started the disasters on Dalna." Avon glanced over her shoulder one last time at her mother, Senator Starros, standing in the midst of the concourse and watching her daughter with an expression somewhere between relief and pride. "I haven't told anyone what happened except Vernestra. She didn't call Starlight Beacon and tell them everything, did she?"

Imri shook his head. "No, there wasn't time."

Avon took a deep breath and then let it out. "So how did my mother know all of that?"

Imri didn't say anything, and he didn't have to. He just patted Avon on the shoulder awkwardly. "Let's find the answer out, together."

✿

Vernestra walked toward her room. All she wanted was a shower and a quick rest in her own bed, and she was halfway there when she was stopped by Jedi Master Avar Kriss.

"Vernestra. Good work helping with the Dalnan evacuation," she said, giving Vernestra a tired smile.

"The Nihil got away, though. It was a Tempest Runner this time. A Quarren by the name of Kara Xoo. And the president of Dalna was apparently working with the Nihil."

"Yes, I know. Maru is interviewing the security chief in my office right now because we want to make sure we have all of the information from him before he gets resettled. But that's not why I came to find you. Vernestra, we have some intel that seems to indicate that the Nihil are gathering at one of their old hideouts. I'm leading one final mission to root them out, once and for all. How would you like to join me?"

Vernestra looked back toward where Avon and Imri were deep in conversation. Sure, they'd managed to save the people of Dalna, but what would happen next time if there weren't any Jedi around. The Nihil were making a comeback, and they had to prevent it however they could.

It was up to Vernestra and the rest of the Jedi to finally, finally stop them in their tracks. And to make sure nothing ever rose from the ashes of their violence.

"When do we leave?"

Justina Ireland is the author of *Dread Nation*, a *New York Times* best seller and YALSA 2019 Best Fiction for Young Adults Top Ten selection. Her other books for children and teens include *Deathless Divide*, *Vengeance Bound*, *Promise of Shadows*, and the *Star Wars* novels *Lando's Luck*, *Spark of the Resistance*, *A Test of Courage*, and *Out of the Shadows*. She enjoys dark chocolate and dark humor and is not too proud to admit that she's still afraid of the dark. She lives with her husband, kid, dog, and cats in Maryland.

You can visit her online at www.justinaireland.com.

ABOUT THE
ILLUSTRATOR

Petur Antonsson is a freelance illustrator for publishing and animation who lives in Reykjavik, Iceland. His full name is Pétur Atli Antonsson Crivello, and he was born and raised in Iceland by his Icelandic mother and French father. He graduated from the Academy of Art University in San Francisco in 2011 with a BFA in illustration. Petur worked in the gaming industry in San Francisco before moving back to Iceland, where he's currently doing freelance illustration work for various clients and companies around the world. He is represented by Shannon Associates.